Miss Darcy's Christmas

Pride & Prejudice Continues
Book 5

Karen Aminadra

Karen Aminadra

Two cousins, one aunt, and a suitor – what could possibly go wrong?

Georgiana Darcy's head is in a spin after being invited to London for the Christmas season.
Thrust into high society, she is overwhelmed by the attention.
Her cousin, Colonel Fitzwilliam, and the dashing Lord Hugh DeVere come to her rescue.
But all is not as it seems. One is goodness himself, while the other has all the appearance of it.
With her head full of love and matrimony, can Georgiana see the gentlemen for who they truly are?
Having dreamt of finding true love, will she accept a match that dazzles on the surface, or dare she strive for a love that fills her heart?

Karen Aminadra

Cover designed by www.stunningbookcovers.com

Karen Aminadra
Visit my website at www.karenaminadra.com

Printed in the United States of America

First Printing: Dec 2018
Flourish Publishing

ISBN: 9781790122790

Thanks

My heartfelt thanks to Brenda and Beverley as always. Love and respect to Katie and Cari for their kind words of encouragement and their advice.

Much appreciation to the talented Daniela at www.stunningbookcovers.com for the wonderful cover art.

And finally, from the bottom of my heart I give thanks to my wonderful husband, always there, always loving, and always full of inspiration.

Contents

One

Miss Georgiana Darcy arrived home to Pemberley, in her brother's carriage, from visiting her aunt, Lady Matlock. She dismounted in a hurry as soon as it stopped, ran up the steps, and in through the front door. Her haste was such that her nimble fingers fumbled with the ribbons as she tried to unfasten her bonnet. She tossed the offending object unceremoniously onto the table in the centre of the entrance hall and ran through the great house towards her brother's study. Only the thought of upsetting him stayed her tongue from calling out his name as she ran, her excitement was so great.

Fitzwilliam Darcy looked up from his work at the desk, his face a picture of concern as Georgiana burst through the door and stood grinning inanely before him. "Whatever is the matter, Georgiana?"

"Oh!" Georgiana panted, out of breath and desperately trying to form her words so she did not sound out of her wits. "Dearest brother, I have the most exciting news."

"So exciting you thought it necessary to run?" His eyebrows rose as he spoke, while he replaced his quill pen in the holder.

Georgiana approached the desk and leant upon it. "I have just this moment returned from visiting with our Aunt Henrietta." She paused to catch her breath.

"Is she well?" Darcy asked as he came around the desk and took hold of his sister's hands, the concern still on his features. "For what are you agitated? Is something wrong?"

Georgiana shook her head. Her soft curls bouncing with the movement. "No, not at all. She is quite well, I assure you. In fact," she grinned from ear to ear, "she has made me a proposal."

Darcy's eyes widened at her declaration. "Oh?"

Georgiana nodded, swallowing to wet her dry throat. "As you know, since our dear uncle died earlier in the year, our poor aunt has suffered greatly."

"That she has. She is only now entering into half-mourning. She has taken Uncle Thomas' death very hard indeed." Darcy let go of his sister's hands and crossed to the drinks table, where she watched him pour her a small glass of wine. "Here, drink this."

Georgiana gratefully took it, sipped slowly, and allowed the liquid to quench her thirst. "Our cousin Thomas and his wife

Eleanor have settled in quite well now as Lord and Lady Matlock."

"Good. I am heartily glad to hear it. An estate as large as theirs needs a seamless transition."

Georgiana watched as he tilted his head towards the open door, his gaze fixed upon it. She strained her ears to listen for what he discerned. Shortly, she heard the unmistakable sound of her new sister-in-law's footfalls coming towards them. She turned around, the grin returned to her face, more than pleased to see Elizabeth Darcy.

"Whatever is going on?" Elizabeth asked as she passed through the door. "I heard a carriage pull up, and then I thought I heard someone running?" Her eyes sparkled as they locked onto Georgiana's, and she stood beside her husband.

"That was me, I'm afraid," Georgiana replied lowering her eyes in shame. She twisted the stem of the glass with her fingers nervously. "I know a lady is not supposed to run, but I was in such a state of agitation."

Gently touching her arm, Elizabeth replied, "It is of little consequence when we are alone as a family, Georgiana. Do not be so hard upon yourself."

Georgiana looked up into her sister-in-law's deep and caring eyes and breathed easily.

"Then do tell us what has you in such agitation," Elizabeth encouraged while absentmindedly rubbing at her swollen belly and standing next to her husband.

Georgiana glanced at Elizabeth's growing girth, and her heart swelled with love at the thought that she and her brother were to have their first child.

"You mentioned our cousins, Lord Thomas and Lady Eleanor Fitzwilliam of Matlock," Darcy prompted.

Shaking her head, Georgiana collected her thoughts. "Yes. Oh, how remiss of me!" She finished off the last drop of wine, handed the glass back to her brother, and continued. "Our aunt, I am afraid to say, is feeling a little out of place now that there is a new mistress in Matlock Hall."

Darcy's head bobbed slowly up and down. "Sadly, that is often the case with a dowager. Soon the dowager's house will be built. I am certain of it."

"That is very sad, though. Is there nothing that can be done?" Elizabeth asked.

"That is what I want to say. Our aunt has the wonderful notion of going to London this Christmas."

"That will be delightfully diverting for her," Elizabeth added.

"Yes, it will be," Georgiana agreed.

"Although," Georgiana watched as Elizabeth's smile slipped as she spoke, "I do not think a widow on her own in London's society is very proper."

With his eyes sparkling and a smile playing on the corners of his mouth, Darcy said, "Not proper at all. But that is not what has got you into a state of agitation, is it?"

Both Georgiana and Elizabeth giggled. Darcy knew her so well.

"No, it is not." She paused before pressing on. "Our aunt has asked if she may have permission to take me with her this Christmas." She knotted her fingers together nervously as Darcy and Elizabeth gazed at each other questioningly. "You will both be at Netherfield with the Bingleys and Bennets," she looked sorrowfully at Elizabeth. "You know how uncomfortable I am around the Bennets."

Elizabeth burst out laughing. Georgiana loved the sound of it.

"Yes, I am aware of how tiring my family is to many people, my dear sister." Elizabeth reined in her laughter.

"Our aunt says it would be diverting for her to introduce me into society now that I'm seventeen years old. She thinks a play or two would do her the world of good," Georgiana added, her eyes locked on her brother's pleadingly.

"Well, what do you say?" Darcy asked, turning to his wife.

"This winter I cannot chaperone Georgiana in society. We all know very well that I shall enter my confinement almost as soon as we arrive at Netherfield Park in Hertfordshire. That would mean Georgiana would have to wait another year before her debut. She would then be eighteen." She shot Georgiana a look filled with mirth. "She shall be a veritable old maid by then."

Darcy said nothing as he watched the repartee. The silence stretched on for what seemed to Georgiana to be an eternity as he thought about his wife's words. They all understood what Elizabeth meant by pointing out that the following Christmas season Georgiana would be eighteen years old. By that age, she would be considered by some in society to be a little old, perhaps even a spinster. Tongues would wag, wondering why she was not married or engaged to be. Even if Elizabeth had meant it in jest, society could be cruel to a young lady, Georgiana knew full well.

She looked down at her hands clenched before her and frowned, feeling the cruelty of such a world that would designate her as unmarriageable by the time she was merely eighteen.

"You are right, as usual, dearest Elizabeth," Darcy replied. "However, I am concerned for your safety." His gaze moved to Georgiana's, and her stomach sank. "Will our aunt be in a fit state to chaperone you in our nation's capital?"

"Oh, Fitzwilliam, this is not only for my benefit but for hers too. Our aunt needs distraction. She needs something to take her mind off her mourning, and introducing me into society is the perfect solution. She knows so many people there and has already discovered which musicians and singers are to perform this year. She is quite as excited as I am."

Darcy's eyebrows knit together. "But I had so hoped...so wished...to introduce you into society myself, with Elizabeth."

Georgiana took a deep breath to say something, but her sister-in-law beat her to it.

Tenderly laying her hand upon her husband's sleeve, Elizabeth spoke, her voice soft and gentle. "Perhaps this way is for the best. I know, my dear, that you do not enjoy balls and assemblies as much as others do. We will both be occupied greatly over the next few months, and Georgiana, at seventeen, is ready to be introduced into society. It would be cruel to make her wait another year."

With bated breath, Georgiana watched the interaction between the married couple. Darcy slowly nodded at her words.

"Your aunt never had a daughter of her own. Having lost her husband earlier in the year must have been the greatest blow she has ever experienced in her life. Let them both take joy in each other's company by allowing Georgiana to go with Aunt Henrietta to London this Christmas."

Darcy inched closer to his wife, lowering his head towards hers. "You are right, as usual," he muttered, placing a kiss on the end of her nose.

"So I can go?" Georgiana's eyes opened wide.

"You may go," Darcy inclined his head. "At Netherfield we shall be but twenty-eight miles from our aunt's house in London. Dispatches can reach us rapidly, and should you need to come to us or send for us to come to you, we can be there within a few hours."

His concern touched her deeply. "Yes, brother," she replied, her voice throaty with emotion.

"So it is decided then," Elizabeth chirped cheerily. "We are to Hertfordshire this Christmas season, and you are to London. I hope you take every opportunity of enjoying yourself."

"I intend to," Georgiana replied, her smile lighting up the room.

Two

Three months later found Georgiana sitting opposite her aunt in her chilly and draughty chaise carriage on their way to London. Sitting beside them were their maids, who hung on every word the dowager said as she wittered away all the while.

"Of course, it was all vastly different in my day," she bemoaned, staring unseeingly out of the carriage window. "The dresses were far more elegant than today's fashions by a long chalk. And I particularly enjoyed wearing a wig rather than having my own hair tugged about and abused as is the mode today." She nuzzled her chin deeper into the black-and-white ermine fur collar on her pelisse. "It was so much nicer to be able to remove it after a long day. Refreshing, I should say. These days one has to put up with a tired head. I am so relieved I am not young now."

Georgiana smiled kindly at her when she caught her aunt's eye.

"But you, my darling niece," she said as a bemused expression brightened her demeanour, "will be the belle of any ball and the toast of London this season, I daresay. You mark my words, Georgiana. Everybody will want to be acquainted with you."

"I do not know about that, Aunt. I am content just to be going to spend Christmas in London with you." Georgiana looked down at her hands, carefully folded in her lap, uncomfortable with such talk. She did not relish the idea of being the centre of attention.

Aunt Henrietta's smile turned indulgent as she accepted the compliment. "Dear Elizabeth looked well, did she not?" she said, changing the subject.

Georgiana nodded in agreement. She had not expected to see Elizabeth looking as spritely so close to her delivery date. Elizabeth and Fitzwilliam departed for Hertfordshire one week before Georgiana travelled south with her aunt. The Darcys had travelled in convoy with Mr and Mrs Collins, the minister and his wife, along with their son, William, following.

As their route took them past Netherfield Park, they sojourned there overnight. Georgiana was overcome to see not only Elizabeth so close to her time but also Jane Bingley, Elizabeth's sister. Georgiana was overjoyed when her brother and his closest friend married the sisters the winter before.

She could not have imagined better matches for the gentlemen than the ones they chose for themselves. It was a delight to spend time amongst them. More than once throughout her own childhood, Georgiana had wished for more siblings. Elizabeth and Jane both treated her as a beloved sister. She cherished their new relationships, and she could tell by the happiness on Fitzwilliam's face that the three ladies getting along so famously brought him great joy.

A hole in the road jolted the carriage and brought her mind back to the present. As her eyes traced the pattern on the material of her aunt's dark grey mourning dress, she wished, *If only I could be half so fortunate as my brother and Elizabeth have been.*

Fitzwilliam Darcy had always been a doting brother to her. Georgiana had never wanted for anything since their father died. Darcy had taken care of everything. He saw to it that she had the best governess he could find and that her education lacked nothing. He indulged her frequently, often buying her gifts and trinkets. She felt blessed to have him as a brother.

Now, after seeing him with his new bride, together not only at Pemberley but at Netherfield Park, Georgiana was more than ever convinced that he was a doting husband too. There was no doubt in her mind he would also be an adoring father.

A smile played around the corners of her mouth at the thought of a new member of the Darcy family. She wondered if Elizabeth would give birth to a girl or a boy. Not that it mattered either way to the married couple, or to her either. The new arrival was excitedly anticipated by all. Fitzwilliam and Elizabeth were still in the midst of the flush of romance that engulfed all newlyweds, and she doubted this would be their only child.

Georgiana admitted to being envious of their love and the romance between them. She was not jealous, for her brother continued to lavish affection upon her and her new sister was all she had ever wanted. However, more than once over the past year her mind had strayed back to a time when she believed she was in love. She knew now it was a passing fancy, a childish folly, but she wished and hoped for true love to come her way. In society, she understood, women rarely had the good fortune to marry for love. She crossed her fingers and prayed she would be one of the lucky ones.

She shifted position, moving her numbing posterior, and watched the scenery pass by outside the window. She knew now how foolish she had been that summer. Her affection for the son of their late father's steward, George Wickham, was nothing more than a fleeting fancy. His easy manners and silver-tongued words were all that convinced her of his ardent love. How wrong she was. After confessing all to her brother in a letter, Darcy had rushed to be by her side. As soon as he arrived, Wickham’s character changed, and he shied away from both her and her brother. She began to see him for what he truly was, a fortune hunter. In the presence of her brother, he no longer kept up the act of being a man head over heels and passionately in love. George Wickham’s prize, she discovered much to her chagrin, was nothing more than her thirty thousand pounds in dowry.

Georgiana sniffed and pursed her lips. *I shan't ever make that mistake again.* She was adamant no man would so easily fool her. She frowned as she thought. *But I am not well acquainted with the world. How shall I ever know if a man truly loves me or simply desires my fortune?*

"Not far now," her aunt, the Dowager Countess, Lady Henrietta Fitzwilliam of Matlock, declared.

"Good," sighed Georgiana's maid, stretching out her back and yawning unbecomingly.

Georgiana shot her a disapproving look.

"Sorry, Miss Darcy," Meg muttered and hung her head.

"Do not fret. It has been a dreary and tiresome journey from Hertfordshire, and I too am tired and in need of stretching my legs a little. If only the rain would stop." Aunt Henrietta sighed and shoved her hands deeper into the ermine muff that lay across her lap. "It's the sort of cold that gets deep into one's bones and refuses to leave. I daresay we shall both be taxing the kitchen staff this evening and ordering hot baths to be drawn in our rooms."

"It has been a terribly harsh summer, and our farmers say all portents point to a harsher winter to come," Georgiana offered.

"Indeed. It does make one wonder what the winter will be like this year. It has been a dreadful year all round." Aunt Henrietta sighed deeply, and Georgiana knew she was thinking about having lost her husband to consumption earlier in the year. "I believe the broadsheet newspapers are declaring that it is the year without a summer."

"I can well believe it. It seemed like spring barely had the strength to change the season and then gave up entirely. I hope things will get back to normal soon enough." Georgiana stretched her toes towards the heated brick in the centre of the floor and was disappointed to find that it had almost grown cold since their departure from Netherfield Park.

"I had thought that, with our removal from Derbyshire to London, our winter would be warmer this much farther south." The old lady leant forward, almost pressing her nose against the windowpane in the door. "It is not so much warmer at all, but I declare it is ever so much drearier, drab," she slumped back in the chair, huffing, "and a darn sight wetter than Derbyshire to boot." She sat back and closed her eyes as she rested her head against the plush upholstery. "I wish I had brought one of my dogs to keep my feet warm." She chuckled. "Perhaps I shall have to purchase one of those lap dogs that are so popular with ladies of the *ton*."

By the time they reached Earl Matlock's house in Pembroke Square, North London, the temperature had plummeted even more and the rain had turned to snow.

As the footman opened the door, Aunt Henrietta declared, "Oh, this is ghastly! Come along, Georgiana! Make haste! Let us get into the house before we catch our death of cold out here."

Georgiana descended the carriage, helped her elderly aunt negotiate her way past the slushy puddles in the street and up the three steps into the house, where the butler held the door open for them.

"It is heartily good to see you, Hobbs," Aunt Henrietta said undoing her bonnet ribbon. "We will need hot water in our rooms and tea in the drawing room as soon as possible. It has been a frightfully chilly journey."

"Yes, ma'am. And might I say, it is good to see you too." Hobbs took their bonnets and pelisses. "I trust you had a pleasant journey from Derbyshire, though, ma'am?"

"It was tolerably good until Hertfordshire, as I said," Lady Matlock informed him, "where, unfortunately, the weather was not on our side. As we neared Watford, the roads were all but an impassable quagmire." She spun around to check that the trunks and maids were now all in from the cold. "Are we all in safe and sound?" she asked. Satisfied that all were accounted for and out of the inclement weather, she turned back to Hobbs. "Get that door closed and get the tea made."

"Yes, ma'am."

"Now," Aunt Henrietta took hold of Georgiana's hand, "come with me, my dear. We are both to be in the front bedrooms. They get the late afternoon sun and, as such, they warm up nicely. Yours is the lavender one." She smiled fondly. "I remember when you were a child, you loved that room the best."

Georgiana tilted her head to the side, recalling with precision the last time she was in that particular room. "You certainly have a good memory, Aunt. It has been an awfully long time since I was last here."

"My dear," she gave Georgiana's hand a little squeeze as they ascended the stairs to the first floor arm in arm, "by the time you get to my grand old age, memories are about all you have left."

"Oh, how very maudlin!" Georgiana turned her head to observe her aunt as they walked along the landing towards the front bedrooms. She did not rightly know her aunt's age. The years had etched lines on her face, yet she did not believe her to be of great age, certainly not as old as her uncle, who died at the grand age of sixty-seven. However old she was, Georgiana admired how soft and velvet-like her skin was. She just resisted the desire to reach out and caress it, its allure was so great. She always remembered her to be a famous beauty, and she still was, even as she aged. "You cannot be of any great age at all, Aunt. Not when your eldest son is only five-and-thirty years old."

To Georgiana's surprise, the great lady by her side burst out laughing. "Oh, my dear niece! What a delight you are!"

Having seen her aunt safely installed in her own room, Georgiana retired to hers. She remembered the way, of course. Memories assaulted her senses as soon as she placed her hand on the knob and opened the door. Vividly, she recalled her mother in this room many years before, with herself and her brother running around and playing tag together happily. A shiver passed across her shoulders as she closed the door behind her, and a profound sadness stirred her heart. She missed her mother and father still after so many years had passed. Neither of them lived, and this time it was Georgiana's turn to be the occupant of this lavishly decorated guest room. She glanced around at the full tester bed and the beautiful bespoke furniture, seeing her mother before each piece in her mind's eye. Her gaze lingered on the dressing table. She had spent many hours as a small child sitting and watching her mother have makeup applied and her long elegant hair styled into the period's fashion. Georgiana's throat constricted.

Shaking her head to rid herself of memories that dragged with them an overpowering and unbearable melancholy, Georgiana walked directly to the front windows and surveyed the street outside. The snow was heavier now and, from what she could see from her vantage point, it was beginning to settle upon the bushes and trees. *If it carries on this way for much longer, the pavement and roads will be covered as well.*

A gentle tap at the door alerted her to what she assumed was her maid's presence. "Come in," she bade, and, as she expected, the young girl opened the door and entered, a footman following closely behind carrying Georgiana's trunk. "Ah, wonderful. Please put it at the end of the bed," she directed, half-turning momentarily and then going back to gazing at the increasingly white scene in the street outside.

The two women waited until the footman had taken his leave before speaking to each other.

"Beggin' your pardon, Miss Darcy, but that was some tiresome journey, an' make no mistake. Do you want to take a nap before tea? I can inform her ladyship if you like."

"I agree with you, Meg. It was tiresome. But we are here now, and we shall not travel again until the first signs of spring." She strode towards the bed and smoothed her hands over the rich damask bedspread. "I would so like to take a nap, Meg, but I fear that if I do, I shan't sleep at all this night." She smiled at the girl who still hovered near the door and still looked half-frozen. "I think we'd best unpack the trunk and see if the exertion cannot warm us both up a little."

Three

By the time Georgiana had changed out of her travelling attire into a morning dress and descended the stairs to the great drawing-room, the fires had already been lit, and she was glad to see the blaze in the chimney warming the room. The orange glow was welcoming, and Georgiana felt the tension from such a tedious journey begin to leave her body. Tea was served and awaited her on the table before the settees, along with a plate of sweet mince pies.

Georgiana had only just poured herself a cup of tea and sat down when the doorbell sounded. She made to place her cup back down on the tray when her aunt raised her hand to stop her.

"Stay where you are. Hobbs will tell whomever it is that we are not at home to callers today. Enjoy your tea, my dear." Her steely grey eyes held Georgiana captive until she sat back down on the settee. "I daresay word has spread throughout town that I have arrived. No doubt, many of my acquaintances and many more genteel folk with whom I am not acquainted shall also be paying their respects. For who does not wish to rub shoulders with nobility when a Dowager Countess comes to stay?" She pressed her lips into a thin line. "Goodness knows it would be polite of them to leave off calling until tomorrow morning at least. Why they feel the need to be the first to call, I shall never understand. It is not as though it carries some sort of accolade with it. I shall be the one to make the decision as to with whom we associate, regardless of who called to see us first."

Georgiana looked over the rim of her cup of tea at her aunt as she sipped and saw her eyes now twinkling in much the same way her brother Fitzwilliam's did. Her tone was scolding and her words complained, but her eyes told how she found the situation amusing all the same.

"Of course, you may also have something to do with it, being the sister of Mr Darcy and all." Aunt Henrietta's giggle was so quiet that one would have missed it unless they were watching her closely. Her shoulders jiggled up and down ever so slightly, as did the bodice of her gown. Her lips remained tightly together to contain her laughter.

"I doubt very much that anyone would wish to see me," Georgiana spoke up.

Before Aunt Henrietta could issue a response, the clearing of a throat alerted them to Hobbs' presence.

"Begging your pardon, ma'am, but already the calling cards are piling up."

"You see, my dear?" Aunt Henrietta addressed Georgiana archly. "Bring them here," she said, waving her hand at Hobbs.

The butler did as he was bid and placed the tray beside the Dowager Countess on the settee. One by one she picked them up, making humming noises or huffing as she read from whom the card was.

"Well, it seems all and sundry have made their intentions known. They are champing at the bit for a visit with us or from us." She tossed the last of the cards back onto the pile beside her and signalled for Hobbs. "Take them away and put them on my writing table for now." She returned to her cup of tea. "I cannot be dealing with invitations to visit or be visited by anyone at the moment. I have such a thumping headache. I do loathe travelling."

"Is there anything you wish me to get you, Aunt?" Georgiana asked, scooting to the edge of her seat.

Aunt Henrietta sipped her tea, her eyes closed. "Oh, you are such a good girl. Such a blessing to my dear sister, Anne," she whispered, almost as though to herself.

Again, memories of her mother flooded Georgiana's mind. Inside, she knew this visit was going to be brimming over with nostalgia. She swallowed down the lump in her throat. *If*

I am to be reminded of my dear Mama, then I shall have to gain control of my own emotions. I deeply miss her, especially at this time of year, and even more so with my first venture into London society. I wish Fitzwilliam and Elizabeth were here. She closed her eyes.

"Why the long face?" Aunt Henrietta asked, jogging Georgiana back to the present.

Shaking her head, her curls bouncing onto her cheeks, she replied, "Oh, it's nothing, Aunt. I was simply thinking of Fitzwilliam and Elizabeth."

"I am sure they are very well just where they are." Aunt Henrietta replied, nodding towards the plate of mince pies. "You really ought to eat something, Georgiana. You are looking decidedly wan. Clearly, travelling does not agree with you either."

"Yes, Aunt. That must be it." Georgiana did as she was told, reached out, and picked up a mince pie from the icing sugar-dusted pile. She put it on a side plate and returned to the settee, glad of the occupation of chewing and not talking. Her emotions were getting the better of her. Thankfully, with each swallow, she felt the lump in her throat lessen.

Instead of following that melancholy train of thought, she focussed her full attention on the pie in her hands. She loved the spicy fruit pies each Christmas and often had to restrain herself from eating more than two of them in one sitting. The pastry was butterier than the ones made by their cook at Pemberley, but she found the addition pleasant. Also, somehow these were sweeter, and, if she was not deceived, these also contained more cognac. She wondered if asking for the recipe would offend Cook. The thought ran through her mind of procuring it and asking Mrs Reynolds, their housekeeper, to see if she could find a way of persuading their cook to give the recipe a try. She licked the icing sugar off her lips. *Either that or I shall have a batch sent to me from Pembroke Square each and every year.*

For Georgiana, mince pies always heralded the beginning of Christmastide, and she was filled with the warmth and joy that accompanied the season as she ate.

Her mind drifted back to Pemberley. In Derbyshire around this time, they were sure to have a light dusting of snow. However, with London's reputation, she believed this Christmas would be dank and wet, the southeast having a reputation for rain. Whether that was true or not, Georgiana could not rightly say, having not travelled much in the region.

She opened her eyes and stared into the orange flickering flames of the fire. *Never mind. Here with Aunt Henrietta, I am certain to have a wonderful time, I have no doubt.*

Four

By the time evening came and dinner was called, Georgiana had written to her brother, bathed, and was so tired from the journey that she was practically falling asleep on the settee before the fire in the drawing room.

She forced her heavy lids to open as Hobbs entered the room and informed her that dinner was served. She pushed hard to move her leaden limbs as elegantly as she could manage out of the room and into Aunt Henrietta's sumptuously decorated dining room.

The breath stuck in her throat as she saw the room for the first time in years. It had been entirely decorated for Christmas with more ornaments than Georgiana ever remembered seeing, even at Pemberley. She was astounded at the quantity of candles, although, thankfully, they were not all lit. The glare would have been unbearable within the confines of the dining room, she surmised. As she crossed the room to stand next to her aunt, Georgiana lightly brushed her hand over the beautiful evergreen foliage adorning the table. She paused to touch one of the bright red berries, not believing it was real with such vibrancy. However, one touch was sufficient to verify it was indeed real.

"This is beautiful, Aunt," Georgiana said, her eyes wide in awe as she reached her side.

Aunt Henrietta turned her face towards Georgiana's, the same awe and excitement displayed there. "It is, is it not? I do love this time of the year and the perfect excuse to decorate our homes with nature's bountiful splendour."

Georgiana pointed. "What is that?"

Turning her head back towards the sideboard, Aunt Henrietta explained, "When our boys were young and at boarding school, your uncle and I travelled extensively throughout the continent of Europe. It was a most eye-opening experience, I can tell you, and something I would recommend to every young person of means. One of our favourite places was Prussia. We visited during wintertime. They bring the most beautiful evergreen trees into their homes and decorate them with apples and roses made of paper and even with lit candles. I was most taken with the tradition and very excited to bring it back with us to Matlock. Unfortunately, with two young boys full of energy at Christmastide when they were home from school, having lit candles on the tree was not a good idea. Your uncle," here she closed her eyes and placed her hand on her heart, "God rest his soul, did not like the tradition at all. With all the expense he laid out in making our estate the beautiful place it is, he was loath to go outside into the grounds and cut down a tree just to decorate the house at Christmas."

Georgiana smiled at the intense happiness on her aunt's face. "And now you have decided that you want to have that particular tradition this year," she replied tentatively.

"Yes. I find my mind stayed upon my dear husband far more these past few days than it has since his passing. Although my thoughts are not turning melancholy, so do not alarm yourself on my account, but they are filled with wonderful memories of our life together."

Georgiana placed her hand upon her aunt's arm.

"So, you see, my dear," Aunt Henrietta patted Georgiana's hand, "I had this little sapling brought inside. He is still in the ground in his little pot, and I intend to keep him well watered so that in the spring, after spending a little time in the orangery, he can go back outside where he belongs."

"It is exactly as it should be."

"Indeed. Your Uncle Thomas would approve, I believe. We can have this tradition wrought with so many happy memories with little or no harm to this tiny tree."

"I think so," Georgiana agreed. "How are you going to decorate it? Not with candles, I presume."

"No." Aunt Henrietta chuckled. "I think prudence wins out as far as candles on the tree are concerned. Besides, I do not believe this little fellow's branches could hold the weight of even a spent candle." She chuckled as she fingered the sapling's branches. "In Prussia we noted that they decorated as a family." She made a funny little noise in her throat and cocked her head to the side, "I suppose they still do. I thought it would be nice if you and I both made little paper roses for it one evening."

Georgiana's smile spread wider. "I would be delighted to help you. It seems to me that it is a beautiful tradition and one I am eager to participate in."

"Thank you, my dear," Aunt Henrietta replied throatily. "I knew you would understand. I do not want to appear overly sentimental in my grief, but I do not see there is anything amiss in surrounding myself with things that spark good, happy memories and make me smile when I remember my Thomas."

"I believe you are quite right, Aunt. You both had a wonderful life together. It is good to remember it, and it is right and proper respect to Uncle Thomas that you do so."

Aunt Henrietta turned and with tears in her eyes, embraced Georgiana. "You are a good girl. You always make me wish I had had a little girl of my own, you know."

As she was released from her aunt's arms, Georgiana replied, "Well, you have me, and you always shall have me."

Clearly fighting against the onslaught of tears that threatened to overcome her, Aunt Henrietta changed the subject. "Shall we eat?"

It was obvious as they ate that both ladies were beyond tired after their journey to London. Their conversation petered away to almost nothing, although their shared love and appreciation for the Christmas season gave them something to chat about when they did speak, until it was time to retire early for the night.

Georgiana hardly remembered climbing the grand marble staircase to her lavender-coloured room. She did not recall undressing and getting into a crisp white cotton nightgown. The one thing she did remember was how delightfully comfortable and soft the bed was to her exhausted body. The feather pillow moulded itself around her head and neck and, not long after, she breathed a sigh of pure pleasure, then fell asleep, a contented smile lingering on her plump lips.

Five

The following morning brought their first real callers. Georgiana thought that all of London's society wanted to be acquainted with the Dowager Countess and her niece. She was not used to being in such high demand, and her stomach filled with the fluttering wings of nervous butterflies.

She had thus far led a fairly sheltered life, and at this moment, holding the door handle of the drawing room, she appreciated how much her brother had protected her. She knew that as soon as she stepped into the room on the other side of the door, she would come under such close scrutiny from countless ladies throughout the morning that she did not know how she would bear it. She couldn't wait for the ordeal to be over, and it had not even begun.

Taking a deep breath, Georgiana pushed open the door and stepped through. Her aunt, the Dowager Countess, sat waiting in her favourite chair beside the fire.

"Oh, good. You're here. Come and sit opposite me. That way I can see you when the visitors call."

Georgiana frowned. "What do you mean, Aunt?" She did as she was asked and sat down opposite.

"We must have a secret code when visitors call. Sometimes it is a necessity for when things get a little tedious." She tapped the side of her nose. "I shall wink at you with my left eye, the furthest away from our guest."

Georgiana's mouth twitched. "Whatever for?"

"Then you will stand and say, 'Aunt, we must make preparations if we are to make our luncheon arrangement.'"

Georgiana covered her mouth as a gasp escaped it. "A deception?"

Aunt Henrietta waggled her head from side to side. "More like a great hefty nudge out the door." Her eyes shone at Georgiana's shocked expression. "I'll let you into a little secret, shall I?"

Georgiana nodded.

"I like less than half of those who will attend on us today, and I would not wish the remainder on my worst enemy." She tucked her chin into her neck. "I can count only a handful of society as friends and even fewer that I would take into my confidence. You shall see what I mean." She played with the onyx beads around her throat. "The quicker we get some of them in and out again, the better, my dear."

Unable to help the grin that spread across her face, Georgiana replied, "Very well, Aunt. I shall keep a watchful eye out for your wink."

"Besides," Aunt Henrietta continued, rearranging her skirts about her knees, "at my age, there is only so much tea one can drink during the course of the morning."

Georgiana snorted and covered her mouth again. "I suppose it is too much to hope that no one comes calling."

"Tish! I doubt anyone in London could resist. Remember who I am." She licked her lips and sucked in her cheeks as she tried to refrain from laughing. "I remember why Thomas and I stopped coming to London now. Neither of us enjoyed feeling like an exhibit in a museum. Before his father died and Thomas became the Earl of Matlock, very few people even gave us the time of day. As soon as he inherited the title, they all came crawling out of the woodwork. We shall greet everyone. Then, once the pleasantries are over and done with, we decide with whom we would like to socialise while we are here. It is a necessary evil, I'm afraid, but it is soon finished."

The doorbell rang, and they both shot a wary glance at the drawing room door.

"Be careful, Georgiana, dear. There are many wolves in sheep's clothing. As your uncle used to say, I wouldn't trust them as far as I could throw them." She took a deep breath. "Still, I intend to find some of society's best for you to associate with. We need to find you one or two beaux to stand up with to dance and perhaps to fall in love with, eh?"

It was with her last words that the door was opened and the first of their guest arrived. Georgiana's face was flushed red as she curtseyed in greeting to Louis Ashton, who it turned out, was a friend of Colonel Fitzwilliam, Aunt Henrietta's younger son.

Georgiana sat quietly throughout and scarcely said anything above "It is a pleasure to make your acquaintance" and "It was lovely to meet you. I hope we shall have the pleasure of meeting again soon."

Not long after Louis Ashton departed, they were joined by Mrs Chamberlain and her three daughters. They had recently returned from India and had much to say on the subcontinent, the climate, and the tedious journey back to England. Georgiana did not think they took a breath the whole visit long.

Following their departure, the two women heaved a great sigh of relief.

"Are they all as draining as that?" Georgiana asked, sipping the last of the tea from her cup.

"Let us hope not," Aunt Henrietta replied, fanning herself with her handkerchief. "What bores they all are!"

There was just enough time for them both to attend to their toilette and have the tea things taken away before the bell sounded again.

This is going to be a very long morning. I am so thankful that our circle was small growing up, Georgiana thought, standing facing the door as more visitors entered the room.

For the remainder of the morning, Georgiana came under such scrutiny that she understood entirely what her aunt meant when she said she felt like an exhibit in a museum.

Only this was worse. Georgiana began to worry if they thought ill of her.

She gripped her hands tightly together in her lap and could hear Elizabeth's voice as she gave her advice before her departure. "Pay no mind to what people say to or about you, sister. What is their opinion? It matters not what they think. You are a beautiful, intelligent young lady whose family love her very much. Nothing else matters."

Under her breath, without being heard, she whispered, "Nothing else matters."

One visitor in particular watched her in such a way as to make her squirm in her chair and wish for an excuse to leave the room. Lady Francesca DeVere, the only daughter of the Duke of Somerset, fairly drooled as she complimented the Dowager Countess on her elegant home and accomplished niece.

Georgiana planted a well-practiced smile upon her face and ignored the discomfort in her cheeks which maintaining such a false smile produced. She astounded herself that, after seven visitors, she could still be polite and courteous. *Elizabeth would be proud of me,* she laughed at herself inwardly, knowing her sister-in-law was always one to respond quickly with a witty quip or two. She did not suffer fools easily, and Georgiana admired that trait. She herself could rarely bring herself to say what was truly on her mind. Sometimes she feared she was far too plain and ordinary. It was Elizabeth's wit and intelligence, as well as her fine eyes, that had first attracted Fitzwilliam to her, or so he confessed. She was a cut above every woman of his acquaintance, he said. As Georgiana listened to Lady Francesca prattle on about the delights of London during the winter season, she wondered if she had any distinguishing features of her own which would attract the attention of a gentleman worthy of her hand in marriage.

Shifting position on the settee, she concluded that perhaps she was not the best person to evaluate her own personality in such a way. She all too readily saw her own flaws. She imagined what Elizabeth would say and knew she would mention her kind-heartedness as well as her gentle spirit. Elizabeth always said she envied those traits in her. Georgiana hid a smile as she realised Elizabeth would also tease her by mentioning that her dowry of thirty thousand pounds would also be seen as a veritable and highly sought-after virtue.

Pushing all thoughts of her own virtues and distinguishing features aside, Georgiana did her best to concentrate in the conversation.

"My brother, Lord Hugh," Lady Francesca turned to Georgiana as though what she said was of particular importance to her, "the third son, takes great pleasure in dancing at balls and assemblies during the season. Do you like to dance, Miss Darcy? I am certain he would be desirous of having such a delightful partner as yourself."

Georgiana felt heat rise and a blush spread from her forehead all the way down to the top of her breasts. *Is this what the winter season is all about in society? Am I now to be paraded in front of all the eligible men in London?* She cleared her throat. "I do certainly enjoy dancing, but I cannot say whether I am a delightful partner or not."

"Oh, fie!" Lady Francesca laughed. "You are too modest." She leant forward. "I shall take you under my wing and make sure you have only the best of dancing partners. It would not do to have your precious little feet trodden on by some great lumbering oaf, now would it?"

Georgiana inclined her head in thanks, but she judged from Lady Francesca's wry smile that she had been insulted with her last comment. She took an instant disliking to the Duke's daughter. From that moment on, Georgiana decided to avoid Lady Francesca and her brother Lord Hugh DeVere if it was at all possible. *Surely London is large enough for the three of us to never need meet,* she surmised.

She looked at Lady Francesca with as close a scrutiny as she herself was beheld. Dressed in the deepest lavender with cream lace accents, she certainly looked like the daughter of a Duke. However, her conversation was not to Georgiana's liking. She was snide and haughty, and Georgiana did not like the way Lady Francesca looked down her nose at nearly everything and everyone, except Aunt Henrietta and Georgiana at the present moment, which she presumed was because she had every intention of flattering them. She supposed the Lady wanted to be friends with those of rank. Georgiana wished she was not descended from noble blood at that point. Anything to avoid a closer acquaintance with Lady Francesca. As she worked her facial muscles harder to smile, she thought, *I wonder what she will say about us when we are not present.*

For the remainder of the visit, which thankfully lasted only a very little longer than the perfunctory fifteen minutes, Georgiana kept her responses as short as she could manage to and threw the conversation back at Lady Francesca with a question each time she was addressed. This had the desired effect of making the Duke's daughter the centre of attention, where, of course, she was more than delighted to be. Relaxing in her seat, Georgiana locked eyes with her aunt. The smallest tilt of the older woman's head conveyed her thanks and appreciation. Lady Francesca was content to talk unaided and unhindered about her favourite subject: herself.

When all the guests had departed, both Georgiana and Aunt Henrietta retired to their rooms. Georgiana attended to her toilette and fought the desire for a nap. She lay down on the chaise and reflected on the morning's visits.

If she were honest with herself, there were a couple of ladies with whom she wouldn't mind having a closer acquaintance; however, one visitor stuck out like a sore thumb. She was determined that Lady Francesca and her brother Lord Hugh DeVere would not be among her friends this season.

She was even bold enough to mention it to Aunt Henrietta when they went out for a walk after luncheon.

Aunt Henrietta chuckled as she walked beside her on the pavement. "Do not be so hasty, Georgiana, dear. You'd be a fool to slight the attentions of the son of a Duke, even if he is the third son, my dear."

Georgiana's stomach lurched at the implication. "I'm aware of his position of birth, but if his sister is anything to go by, I really..." She could not finish the sentence but waved her hand in the air and puffed out her cheeks.

"Nonsense!"

She had never heard such a hard tone from her aunt before.

"Do not be so obstinate and headstrong! I declare, I have no idea where you get that from."

She shot her aunt a sideways look and caught the scowl on her face.

"From the way you are reacting, anyone would think you had been told you had to marry the man, for goodness sake. Just be polite to him and dance with him should he ask you to. He is the son of a Duke and related to the King, remember."

As they rounded the corner and walked through the gates to an immaculately kept walled garden, Georgiana clenched her teeth. Her aunt was right; yet inside she wanted to scream. "I know you are right, but did you not say that we should whittle out those we did not wish to associate with? Well," she set her jaw, "I do not wish to associate with the DeVeres."

Aunt Henrietta stopped walking and turned to face Georgiana. She lifted her hand to shield her eyes from the glare of the low winter sun shining brightly that day. "You have had your say and made your point. Now I shall make mine. You could go a long way in England without finding the equal of the DeVeres."

Georgiana made to protest, but the older woman held up her forefinger to stop her speaking.

"When we are in society, attending balls, assemblies, plays, and the like, you shall…we *both* shall pay the DeVeres kind attention. It is obvious that you have taken an instant disliking to Lady Francesca, and I don't blame you. She is a self-obsessed spoilt little rich girl, who, most likely, gives our class a bad reputation. I doubt there is a generous bone in her body." She lowered the finger and softened her tone. "And yet, she is a station or two above us both, my dear. Unless the Prince Regent himself were to entertain us with his presence, we would be foolish not to consider her friendship as both fortuitous and beneficial. I wish the best for you this season, and she will help procure it. Of that I am certain."

Chagrined, Georgiana had no comeback or response. She closed her eyes and nodded slightly, letting her aunt know she was right.

"Dukes are the highest-ranking peers below the Royal Family. Your cousin, the now Earl Matlock, and I, as the Dowager Countess, are somewhere in the middle." She tilted her head to the side, and her grin lit up her face to match the sun beaming on it. "I too would like to rub shoulders with those higher up the ranking than myself. Who knows? We might even get an invitation to St James' Palace this visit if we keep in with the right crowd, if you know what I mean."

Georgiana sighed. "Yes, Aunt. I know what you mean, and I apologise. I was being impudent and childish. As you said, I do not have to be the best of friends with Lady Francesca and I most certainly do not have to marry her brother, who, more than likely, is just as spoilt as his sister."

Aunt Henrietta began to stroll again, linking her hand through Georgiana's arm. "That's the spirit, my girl. We're meant to be having fun here, after all."

Georgiana took a deep breath as they walked on in silence.

"I have an idea," Aunt Henrietta spoke at last. "Why don't we do a little shopping? I still have a gift or two to buy."

Georgiana broke out into a grin. "Let's!"

Six

By the time the sun set that early evening, the temperature had plummeted and the skies threatened a downpour and possibly sleet. Georgiana sighed as she stared out of the window in the drawing room.

"It was such a beautiful day."

"It is winter, my dear. We cannot expect sunshine all the year long." Aunt Henrietta came up beside her. "Perhaps now might be a good time to lighten our spirits by making those paper roses for the tree."

"Yes," Georgiana beamed. "That would please me, Aunt. Let's do that."

"I have paper that I put by years ago to do rainy-day things with the boys." She turned and led the way out of the room towards the study. "Of course, boys being boys, they were not too interested in crafting but in chasing each other around the house, making all sorts of racket as they pelted up and down the stairs."

Georgiana could not help but giggle at the image of her two elegant and grown-up cousins pelting around like little scamps.

She discovered that her aunt had put by more than a few things. She had a whole box full of craft items in one of the cupboards beneath the walnut bookcases.

"Aunt, there is so much to choose from," she said, bending down and picking out a cheery red scrap of paper. "This is lovely."

"I used to make all sorts of things when I was younger. My father used to say I was a fiddler," she explained, lifting the box and carrying it over to the desk. "I could never keep my hands still. They had to have some kind of occupation. So I made things."

Georgiana looked at her aunt's long slender fingers, now showing the crooked signs of aging, and watched as she fiddled with a tiny scrap of tissue paper until it resembled the tiniest of rosebuds. "Oh, that is beautiful," Georgiana gasped. "You have such a talent."

With a contented smile planted on her face, Aunt Henrietta sat down in the chair behind the desk. "I doubt very much that it shall ever be listed as one of my accomplishments."

Georgiana laughed and watched her fingers carefully as they manipulated another piece of paper, endeavouring to copy the Dowager. "I shall remember it always, Aunt."

She looked up and caught her gaze. "Then that is all that matters."

After an hour, Georgiana's eyes began to tire in the candlelight. "I think I need to stop for today."

"Yes, I agree. It would be better to continue when there is more light, although I doubt we need many more decorations." Aunt Henrietta rose stiffly. She nodded at the little pile of things Georgiana made. "I very much like those little bells. What a clever idea." She grinned at her niece. "Let's go to the drawing room and call for tea."

Arm in arm, the pair of them walked through the double doors to the spacious room together. Both stopped dead in their tracks, instantly recognising the dashing man warming himself before the fireplace.

"Oh!" Aunt Henrietta declared, her hands flying to her mouth. "Is it truly you, my son?"

The young man turned, his face lighting up at the sight of the two women in the doorway. "Mama!" he cried out and crossed the space between them in but a few long-legged strides.

As he enfolded her in his arms, Aunt Henrietta wept. "It has been so long since I last set my eyes on you, Richard dearest."

"You too are a sight for sore eyes, Mama," he responded, kissing her silver-flecked hair.

Georgiana watched the pair and, when her cousin Colonel Richard Fitzwilliam finally let her out of the embrace, Aunt Henrietta held him firmly by the arms.

"You look wan."

Richard laid is head to the side and smiled indulgently. “You say that every time I come back from war.”

“Well, it is what I think. I worry. I’m your mother. I’m supposed to worry,” she countered, picking a little fluff off the collar of his jacket.

Again he kissed her tenderly. “I am heartily glad to see you, Mama,” he whispered.

Reluctantly, she stepped aside. “Do you not recognise your cousin?”

Looking up, Richard beheld Georgiana.

She shuffled her feet, uncomfortable with the scrutiny of his stare.

A grin broke out on his face. “Has it been so long that I now behold a grown woman in the place of my young cousin?”

Georgiana felt her face burn and averted her eyes.

“Richard!” Aunt Henrietta cried, playfully cuffing his left arm. “Do not embarrass her so!”

“I apologise, Mama, but my sentiments were genuine. I am all astonishment to find such a pleasant change in you, Georgiana.” He bowed.

Georgiana looked up momentarily into his warm, mid-brown eyes and saw only sincere affection there. She responded to his bow with a curtsey. “I am delighted you have returned home safely from the Iberian Peninsula.”

He inclined his head. “Thank you. I am delighted to be home.” He stepped aside. “Come on in and sit by the fire, both of you.” After seeing them seated, he continued, “It will interest you, Mama, to know that, in the hopes of finding you there, I travelled directly to Netherfield Park to see Darcy."

"Oh!" Aunt Henrietta exclaimed. "We missed each other by a mere couple of days."

"How fares everyone there?" Georgiana asked, unable to keep quiet upon hearing where he'd been.

"Everyone is in the best of health, I assure you. And," he dug his hand into his jacket and produced a letter from inside the pocket, "I have a letter for you from your brother."

In her excitement, Georgiana almost snatched the missive from her cousin's hand. She tore open the wax seal bearing the Darcy family motif and read hungrily.

Aunt Henrietta and Richard watched her as she read.

Georgiana let out a squeal of delight, instantly covering her mouth with her hand. "Did you know?" she looked directly at Richard.

He nodded, chuckling at the same time. "Yes, I did."

"What is it?" Aunt Henrietta demanded.

Georgiana gazed at her aunt, her eyes filling with tears. "Elizabeth has been safely delivered of a baby boy."

Aunt Henrietta clapped her hands in glee. "Oh, wonderful tidings!"

"They have named him William Bennet Darcy," Georgiana declared, clutching the letter to her heart. "I am an aunt!"

"You are indeed, and a finer one no nephew could ever ask for," Aunt Henrietta declared. "Congratulations, my dear."

"I must write to them immediately." She rose and scooted out of the room. She made it to the stairwell before catching herself up short and returning to the drawing room. "I apologise. In my haste and excitement, I forgot." She swallowed and looked straight at her cousin. "Thank you, Richard, for bringing me this letter. You cannot know what it means to me."

"I think, by the expression on your face, cousin, that I can guess." He bowed his head. "You are most welcome. I am heartily glad for you all."

"Thank you," Georgiana replied, spinning on her heel and scampering away, up the stairs and directly to her room. Once there, she devoured every word her brother wrote. He told of Elizabeth's difficult labours, which brought a tear to Georgiana's eye. However, the midwife was on hand and, with her recommendations, Elizabeth gave birth to a healthy baby boy.

Tears dripped from her eyes as she read;

> *...both Elizabeth and our little William are quite well. Elizabeth sends you her warmest regards and promises to write as soon as she is recovered.*

"Oh, how I wish I was there with you all," she lamented, wiping her face dry. Then, instantly remembering her difficulty with Mrs Bennet, she was content to be where she was. She continued to read. Fitzwilliam turned his attention to her and issued advice for her stay in London.

> *...I have entreated our cousin Richard to act as a chaperone should our aunt not be desirous of escorting you. We do not wish to tire her unnecessarily. Richard was more than happy to accept the responsibility. I hope you agree, sister.*

Georgiana smiled at his words. "Despite your own concerns, you have time to think of my well-being." She hurried to the writing table and penned a response. She wanted to send her congratulations as expediently as possible and to tell them that all fared well in London.

* * *

Richard stretched out his long legs as he reclined on the settee. "I'm happy to see you looking so well, Mama," he said, watching her closely.

"What did you expect to find?" Her eyebrows arched. "That I was wallowing in my grief?"

"I didn't mean—"

"I know what you meant," she interrupted. "I know full well that your father would not approve of such comportment. No matter how deeply I wish to lock myself away and weep all day and night, it will not do." She raised her chin defiantly. "When we meet again in Heaven, he will want to know what he missed, and I shall have to fill him in. I can't very well do that if all I do is cry, can I?"

Richard's eyes traced the outline of the face he loved so well.

"I miss him so profoundly, I cannot breathe some days," her voice faltered. "He was a good man."

"That he was. The very best," Richard agreed.

He watched his mother compose herself and then ask, "So, tell me, is the war at an end?"

"For now," he replied. "Napoléon has been captured after being defeated at Waterloo. He is being held on the island of Saint Helena."

"And where is that?" she creased her forehead as she asked.

"It's just off the coast of Africa, Mama."

"Of course," she nodded rapidly. "He escaped from an island before. Is that wise?"

Richard splayed his hands, happy to hear his mother back to her old self. "That is not my decision to make, I'm afraid."

"Well..." She shook her shoulders and cleared her throat. "Let's hope the brute stays put, shall we?"

"Indeed."

"And what of your Spanish beauty?" She held him captive with her steely grey eyes.

"Always direct and to the point, Mama," Richard responded, recoiling from the direct assault on his personal affections.

"A mother has a right to know, Richard," her gaze remained steady and unyielding.

"She married a *vizconde* from Andalusia last month." His response was curt, revealing his bristling feelings.

"Vith...what?"

Richard watched as his mother's perfectly arched eyebrows rose almost to her hairline. "It means viscount in Spanish."

"Well, why didn't you say so?" She clicked her tongue on the roof of her mouth impatiently.

He laid his head on the cushioned back of the settee and closed his eyes.

"Why?"

The word hung in the air, pointing an accusing finger at him.

"Was she of loose morals?"

His eyes snapped open. "Mother!"

"Then give me a logical explanation as to why this foreign woman would see fit to jilt my son for another man." Her lips pursed together, and he knew she would not let the subject drop without a satisfactory answer.

Thankfully, he was spared any more torture by the reappearance of Georgiana. Her face was bright and glowing. He could tell she'd been crying, but her smile spoke volumes about them being tears of joy.

"Georgiana," he stood as he greeted her. "I trust all is well."

"Quite well, I assure you." She treated him to a beautiful smile that gladdened his heart. "I wrote a response to Fitzwilliam's letter. I have just this moment handed it to Hobbs."

"He will be delighted to receive it, I am sure." He held out his hand and guided her to a seat beside the fire. *She truly has grown up in my absence. I am astonished at the change,* he thought.

With Georgiana's arrival, the topic of conversation moved on to more congenial things. He was relieved to have been spared having to give the details of his courtship with Doña Rocio to his inquisitive mother.

* * *

Despite being eager to be reunited with his mother, Richard was somewhat relieved when, after dinner, she retired to her room early, complaining of being overtired.

He offered Georgiana his arm and walked her back to the drawing room and rang the bell. "Let's get this fire stoked up and some brandy inside us. There is a rather nasty chill in the air tonight."

"Yes, there is," she replied, as a shiver ran across her shoulders. He watched her delicate hands pull her shawl tighter around herself. "I confess that I find London to be colder and damper than I presumed it to be."

"It does rain a lot in London," he replied, pouring two glasses of brandy.

"So I see," she giggled.

Richard watched her sip from the glass cupped in both hands, wondering whom she took after the most—her mother or her father. He could see the unmistakable Darcy brow and strong eyes, but her delicate cheeks, nose, and mouth, he was convinced resembled his late aunt, Lady Anne Darcy.

"You really look like your mother, you know," he spoke without thinking. He watched as a blush started at her cheeks and spread its way across her face.

"Apart from my eyes. Fitzwilliam says we have the same eyes, our father's."

"Yes," he nodded in agreement. "You are both unmistakably Darcys."

Georgiana reddened deeper still.

"Have you ventured out into society as yet?"

"No," she replied.

"If Mama is up to going out tomorrow, how about I take you both to an assembly."

Georgiana's face lit up. "I'd love that," she said, excitement dripping off every word.

"Then it is settled. Tomorrow we shall dance."

Her grin spread even wider as the maid arrived to stoke up the fire.

Richard held back his questions, as curious as he was about this new woman in the place of his childlike cousin, while the servant was present. She did her job quickly, and the fire was loaded with logs and crackling away when he finally spoke. "Are you well?"

Georgiana looked across at him, her brows knitted together as one. "As you see, yes. Thank you."

Richard shook his head, unsure of how to form the query on his mind. "No," he shuffled to the edge of his seat. "I am pleased to know you are well, but that was not the aim of my enquiry." He rubbed at the sides of his mouth and watched her patient expression as she continued to gaze at him. "I...I was referring to..." he cleared his throat. "You know...since..."

He watched her features and body tense slightly.

"You mean since Mr Wickham?"

Her voice had a hard edge to it which he did not like at all.

"Yes, since your disappointment."

His stomach sank as he watched her take a deep breath and close her eyes as though taming her temper and counting to ten. "I shouldn't have said a word. I'm sorry, cousin."

"No," her eyes flipped open. "Do not apologise, Richard. I suppose it is natural for you to ask. You are in my and my brother's confidence and know it all."

"But I do not wish to cause you pain by opening wounds if they are not healed."

She studied his face, then the corners of her mouth lifted. "Speaking of wounds, how is yours?"

Richard flexed his left arm and rotated it in the socket. "All well, as you see." He grinned. "It pains me from time to time when the cold penetrates deep into the bone, but most of the time I forget it entirely."

"I am pleased to hear it." Her eyes sparkled for a second before she took another deep breath and answered his first question. "It is something I shall regret for the remainder of my days, I daresay."

"That you were discovered and unable to marry?" The pain that flashed in her eyes made his heart falter momentarily.

Georgiana looked down at the glass she still cradled in her hands. "No." She shook her head. "Not that we are unmarried. That would have been an unhappy union and one which I would have lamented always."

Richard barely breathed.

"What I regret is that I was so persuaded that I was in love."

"You were not?" he frowned.

"Not at all," she said before sipping the amber liquid. "The idea of being in love is so bewitching and ensnaring that, as a young girl with a head full of fanciful thoughts, I was only too ready to be seduced—by love, by Wickham, but mostly by the illusion and feeling of falling in love."

Richard hung his head. Her words struck him in his innermost heart. "I know what you mean."

"You do?"

"Yes," he replied, his voice faltering. "I fancied myself in love with a woman who I not only could not have, but whose goodness and character bewitched me, as you say."

"I did not know this. Was it the Doña in Spain?" she leant forward, her face a picture of concern.

"No," he shook his head. "I have made the same mistake twice. I shall not name her, but I thought I was in love. I even tried to persuade her to leave her husband and run away with me."

Georgiana's hand rushed to her mouth as a tiny gasp escaped her mouth. "Truly?"

"Truly. I was such a fool." He finished his drink and placed the glass on the table before them. "Then in Spain I was beguiled by Doña Rocio's beauty."

Slowly, Georgiana nodded.

"I would have married her. I would have been a good husband to her." He flexed his neck. "But she knew neither of us were in love."

"I am sorry," Georgiana whispered.

"Do not be, cousin. We are brought up to believe that we *must* marry at all costs. As the youngest son, I knew my portion would be small indeed. When I rescued Doña Rocio from being executed for helping the resistance against Bonaparte's army, she bestowed a small fortune on me. It was then that my infatuation began." He held her gaze, hoping she would see the compassion in his eyes. "I too have been foolish."

Her mouth twitched in what he interpreted as a smile. "Then let us learn our lesson. We shall never be so foolhardy again."

"Agreed." Richard nodded and rose as he spoke. He refilled his glass and returned to the seat opposite his cousin. "And yet," he said, swigging the brandy, "one of the main purposes in bringing you here is to *display* you as eligible, is it not?"

Georgiana laid her head to the side and huffed through her nose. "Indeed, it is."

Richard chuckled at her exasperation. "Fed up of it already?"

She wrinkled her nose. "I did not particularly like the visits. I felt like a curiosity in a shop window."

Richard burst out laughing. "Yes, it is a little like that, isn't it?" He watched as she finished the last drop in her glass. "Any takers yet?"

The scolding look she shot him started him laughing again.

When he escorted her to her room much later, he vowed he would protect her against anyone who did not wish to marry her for anything other than the deepest and most ardent love.

Seven

Georgiana was overjoyed the next morning when Aunt Henrietta declared she would be delighted to attend an assembly. Richard brought it up as quickly as he could. Georgiana almost choked on her toast when Aunt Henrietta said yes. She stared down at the white linen tablecloth with a pink rosebud motif, trying not to cough and not wishing her aunt to see the excitement in her eyes.

"Hmm...that would be wonderful," the Dowager declared, putting down her teacup. "I crave to see young Georgiana here dancing and enjoying the amusements London has to offer. The weather has been frightful since we arrived. We have only ventured out of doors to walk in the park. Would you like to go?" She turned to Georgiana.

"Oh," Georgiana responded, "yes, I think it would be a splendid idea." She glanced at her cousin, whose face declared he was moments away from laughing at her discomfort. "Thank you for the invitation."

To his credit, Richard controlled his facial muscles far better than she did. Georgiana was impressed.

"You're welcome. Now that I'm here, I shall do everything in my power to make certain you ladies are entertained."

This time, Aunt Henrietta laughed. "Oh, Richard! We do not need entertaining, but," her eyes darted to Georgiana's, "your cousin needs introducing to the *ton*. Let's be sure and do it correctly." Her gaze returned to her son. "Do not take us to one of those assemblies that your officer friends frequent. They drink far too much for propriety."

"Of course, Mama," Richard appeared chastened, as though the mirth had fled the room with her comment.

"I cannot abide such lack of self-control. A gentleman ought to know how to handle his liquor without it carrying off his head and manners with it."

"You are right, Mama."

"Take us to one where there will be lots of young people Georgiana's age."

Richard stared at his cousin, and she fought the urge to shrink away. "I think I know just the place. Leave it to me."

"And we will not stay out too late," Aunt Henrietta continued as she tucked into her pan-fried kippers. "I find these days that I cannot stay awake as well as I used to."

Georgiana wiped at the corners of her mouth. "I am certain that Cousin Richard will have both our best interests at heart, Aunt."

"Indeed, I will."

Georgiana watched as he reached across the table and gave his mother's wrist a little squeeze.

The dowager looked up at him, her eyes watery, and whispered, "You're a good boy, Richard."

Georgiana saw the tiniest tensing in Richard's jaw and surmised he did not like being called a boy. She could not blame him. After all, he had seen his fair share of bloodshed in battle. Her eyes travelled to his injured shoulder and her breath caught in her throat as she traced the curve of his muscles. *There is nothing boyish about him at all.*

* * *

Dressed in a sprigged muslin dress she had made in the summer and brand-new pumps, Georgiana stepped in through the front doors of the assembly rooms on Montague Street. She held on to Richard's arm as though her life depended upon it while Aunt Henrietta took the other side.

The first thing to assault her senses was the heat, from not just the exorbitant number of candles burning but also from the mass of bodies pressed into the confines of the building. Secondly, Georgiana recoiled from the melange of perfume and colognes that assailed her nostrils. She raised her hand and covered her nose.

"It is a little much, isn't it?" Richard leant towards her and whispered. "Some people need to learn to use scents sparingly."

Glad for her hand over her mouth, Georgiana chuckled at her cousin's comment. "I do hope they keep the doors open; otherwise, more than one lady might faint from the heat."

"I do not remember it being this hot in my day," Aunt Henrietta complained.

Richard snorted. "Mama! It was hotter in your day! Your dresses were heavier, and you all had wigs on."

Snapping her fan open, she caught him playfully on the arm with it. "Yes, well," she replied, her eyes telling he was right. "Set me down somewhere with the other mamas. I want to see Georgiana is well attended, but I do not wish to be in this fray, Richard."

"Very well, Mama," he replied, carefully steering them towards a settee to the side of a grand fireplace which was thankfully unlit.

Georgiana stood by with her aunt while Richard gallantly hunted down the master of ceremonies and persuaded two matrons to scoot along the settee a little, thereby making enough room for his mother to be seated.

They were unimpressed by his request until he happened to drop into the conversation that his mother just happened to be the Dowager Countess of Matlock. Their countenances changed immediately, being only too happy to oblige the wife of the late Earl Matlock and share the settee with such an esteemed personage.

Once the master of ceremonies had made the introductions, Richard left the women to chat and went in search of something to drink.

Georgiana felt his absence immediately. She felt safe in the throng while holding on to his arm. As soon as he departed, she felt bereft and lost, unsure of what to do.

She endeavoured to focus on the conversation the ladies were having, but they were asking Aunt Henrietta about Matlock in Derbyshire, and Georgiana had nothing to contribute to that discussion. She was also loath to butt in and tell them who she was. So in the end she turned about and watched the couples dancing through the archway which separated their salon from the ballroom.

Feeling self-conscious that she was not dressed as elegantly as some of the ladies present, Georgiana inched towards the archway, mesmerised by the rhythm of the dancers.

She started when someone spoke by her ear.

"I cannot tell you how delighted I am to see you here this evening, Miss Darcy."

Georgiana's stomach sank, instantly recognising the voice. She turned, a smile planted firmly on her face. "Lady Francesca, the pleasure is mine, I assure you."

Both the ladies curtseyed eyeing up each other's dresses and hair.

Lady Francesca leant forward and whispered, "You really must permit me to take you shopping, my dear. We cannot have you running around London dressed like a country bumpkin. The fashions here are vastly different to those in Derbyshire."

Georgiana forced the smile to remain in place as she rose from the curtsey. "You are too kind."

"But of course," Lady Francesca smiled, reminding Georgiana of the paintings of snakes she'd once seen in a gallery.

The Duke's daughter stepped aside and there, behind her, was the most handsomely dashing man Georgiana had ever seen.

"Miss Darcy, please permit me the honour of introducing you to my brother, Lord Hugh DeVere."

Georgiana's curtsey was feeble as her knees weakened beneath her. "My lord."

"Miss Darcy, you cannot know what a pleasure it is to finally meet you. My sister has talked of nothing but the enchanting Miss Darcy since visiting you and your aunt."

He reached out and took hold of her hand. Her heart fluttered in her breast as his lips brushed the back of her silk glove.

"Oh, really?" she stammered.

"Hugh, honestly!" Lady Francesca interjected. "He does like to embarrass me." She lowered her voice. "But I do have to admit to being very much taken with you since our first encounter, Miss Darcy. I very much hope we shall become so much better acquainted."

"As do I," Lord Hugh added, his eyes fixed on Georgiana's face.

She knew that it was the intensity of his stare that increased the temperature in the room and compelled her to gasp for air.

"Miss Darcy, if I may be so bold as to ask, might I have your hand for next dance?" His face spoke of his hope. "Unless, that is, you are otherwise engaged."

Georgiana opened her mouth, but no sound came out. She cleared her throat and took in a deep breath. "I am not engaged, my lord."

"Jolly good! And that's enough of the *my lord* nonsense. You can call me Hugh, like all my friends do."

Georgiana gazed up into his face. She liked his features. Not only was he handsome, but she could easily read his feelings on his face. She liked that in a person. Past experience had taught her not to believe a silken-tongued devil. Hugh DeVere, she suspected, was not the self-centred oaf she had presumed he was. So far, she admitted to herself, she liked him very much indeed.

At that moment, the music fortuitously ended and couples flooded from the dance floor.

"Now is our chance, Miss Darcy."

Georgiana realised Hugh still held her hand. As he led the way through the arch, she felt her cheeks and neck burning and knew her face shone red.

Hugh kept his eyes on her, and his smile sent her pulse racing.

* * *

Richard pushed his way through the heaving crowds of people, carefully trying not to spill a drop of the two glasses of punch he carried. When he arrived back at the settee upon which his mother sat, he could not see Georgiana.

He looked about him in a panic. *Darcy will skin me alive if anything untoward happens to his sister,* he thought.

"Do not worry yourself, Richard, dear," his mother called out over the din. "Georgiana is dancing with Lord Hugh DeVere." She pointed in the direction of the ballroom. "There! You can see them. Do they not make a handsome couple?"

"Indeed they do, Lady Matlock."

Richard looked at the woman next to him, nonplussed.

"Let me introduce you to Lady Francesca DeVere, the daughter of the Duke of Somerset."

Richard bowed deeply, unsure what to do. "My lady," he said, keeping his tone as neutral as he could.

"Lady Francesca," his mother continued, "this is my son, Colonel Fitzwilliam."

"I assure you that your cousin is in the safest of hands with my brother, Colonel," Lady Francesca drawled.

"I should hope so," he snapped, his eyes darting to where his view of the couple dancing was obscured by another pair in the set. His hand involuntarily clenched at the glass in his hand, meant for Georgiana. He turned back to the lady before him. "Would you like a beverage, Lady Francesca?"

At the look of pleasure and delight on her face, Richard handed over the glass. He watched her as she drank from it, taking in deep breaths to push away the suspicion that tried to rise inside him.

Darcy had asked him to take good care of his sister, but Richard could not account for the strength of the desire to protect her that washed over him.

His eyes found their way back to the couple dancing. He watched Lord Hugh like a hawk.

"Do you like to dance yourself?" Lady Francesca asked, rising and sidestepping a little nearer to him.

Richard looked down at her. He knew her sort. He knew what she was about. He also believed he knew her brother by reputation, and he would, by far, rather have Georgiana dancing with a python than DeVere. "I have been known to enjoy a dance or two."

Lady Francesca, he noted, treated him to her most endearing smile. "Then I hope that this occasion will be one of them."

"Do you wish to dance, Lady Francesca?" he asked, a thought occurring to him. "May I?" he held out his hand before she had the chance to reply.

Once she took hold of it, Richard pulled her a little inelegantly rather than led her to the dance floor and together they joined a set.

If she is going to dance with him, then I will damn well get as close to them as I can. Richard's thoughts ran hot, and he worked at keeping his face as pleasant as possible, smiling at Lady Francesca each time he caught her eye—which was far more frequently than he liked.

Let him dare put one toe out of line, Richard fumed inside.

* * *

The pace of the dance left Georgiana with scarcely any breath left to converse with Lord Hugh. She thanked heavens for small mercies, as she flushed red each time the man looked into her eyes or spoke to her.

"Have you been to the ballet yet, Miss Darcy?" he asked the next time he passed close enough for her to hear him.

Instantly, Georgiana's eyes lit up. She had only once seen the ballet when Darcy took her to Stratford-upon-Avon. She had loved every minute of it. "Oh, I would dearly love to see the ballet again." She glanced up at him, mesmerised by his eyes as blue and as profound as the deepest ocean.

"Then I shall have to procure us a box," he replied, grinning.

The few seconds she had to wait to speak with him again were agonising as they danced the next part. She walked behind the other gentleman in their set, smiling amiably as she passed him, until she was by Lord Hugh's side again. "I should like that very much, Hugh."

Georgiana thought that the smile on his face was far brighter then than all the candles in the assembly room put together.

"I shall take the liberty of calling on you at the Dowager Countess' house as soon as I have the details of when we shall go to the ballet."

She was aware that her smile matched his at the anticipation. As the white plastered walls with gold-accented agapanthus leaf moulding whizzed past them while they danced, Georgiana thought how mistaken she had been in the DeVeres. *I had not thought to find Hugh as affable as he is. He is quite charming.* They moved down the room and out of the corner of her eye, she could see they were being admired. She was grateful for her dance lessons.

They spun around the room, and Georgiana felt a little dizzy. She did not know if it was from the dancing or from the man with whom she danced. When they passed close to the archway leading from the outer salon, she caught a glimpse of her cousin Richard leading Lady Francesca to dance. *I wonder if even my opinion of Lady Francesca will be a little softened by my knowing her better?*

Just as Richard and Lady Francesca joined a set lower down the room, Georgiana caught sight of his expression. She had to take a second look over her shoulder while she continued to dance. She frowned, not understanding what she saw. His face was like thunder.

"Are you well?" Hugh spoke into her ear.

"Y...yes," she faltered. "I thought I saw your sister dancing with my cousin, that is all."

He laughed. "Why would that make your countenance fall so? My sister is an excellent dancer."

She shook her head once. "I didn't mean..."

Again, he laughed. It was a warm sound that spread though her entire being. "Then what is it?"

"I thought my cousin did not wish to dance," she lied.

"Oh, is that all!" he replied as they separated again to dance with the other couple in the set.

She kept silent after that, ashamed she had told an untruth. However, at every opportunity she looked for Richard. She hoped she was mistaken, but he glowered at Hugh and she detected a scowl to his mouth. *Surely, he is not put out that I danced first with Hugh and not him. How could I have refused to dance with him?*

Georgiana refocused her attention on enjoying the dance, so not to draw Hugh's questions again.

I sincerely hope Richard is not offended.

* * *

Of course, Richard was offended. He could not wait for the dance to end. Thankfully, his partner danced well enough for his concentration and attention to drift to her brother. *The sooner I get my cousin away from him the better,* Richard thought. As the music ended, there was a burst of applause and the sets broke up.

He led Lady Francesca back through the arch to where his mother sat contentedly chatting away with the other mamas.

"Do you wish for more punch, Lady Francesca?" he asked, hoping that his duty was over.

"Thank you, but I am not in need of refreshment," she beamed.

"Very well," he bowed slightly, turned, and spied a friendly face beating his way through the crowd towards him.

"There you are Fitz!" the young man called out as he slapped Richard on the arm.

"Alex! I did not know you were in town."

Alexander pulled a face. "And miss the opportunity of helping you get your sweet little cousin hitched to a rich bachelor?"

Richard scowled. "That is not why we are here."

"Oh, I touched a nerve, eh?" Alexander's smile slipped from his face. "I apologise."

"Are Louis and George here?" Richard changed the subject.

"Too right they are. And winning at the card tables, no doubt." Alex snorted.

They were interrupted when Lord Hugh escorted Georgiana back to them and bowed. "I shall return post-haste with some refreshments, Miss Darcy."

Both Richard and Alexander watched him leave.

"We'll have to do better than that," Alexander whispered in Richard's ear before turning to Georgiana. "I don't suppose you remember me."

Her face was blank.

"I believe you were but six years old the last time I saw you, and I believe I pulled your plaits, for which I apologise," he chortled.

"Oh," she replied, her eyes enlarging.

Richard stepped in with an explanation. "This is my old school fellow, Alexander Salisbury."

He watched as Georgiana curtseyed. His chest swelled with pride seeing her so full of grace and elegance. *She would not be out of place at St James' Palace amongst royalty.*

"I am pleased to see you again, then."

"As am I. It has been too long," Alexander replied. "I always remember holidays in Matlock fondly."

Georgiana smiled. "Yes, my aunt is an excellent hostess."

"Is she here?" He shot a look at Richard who nodded. "Then I must give her my regards." He bowed. "Please excuse me, Miss Darcy."

Richard was left with his cousin, while Lady Francesca hovered expectantly behind them. "I do have other friends I wish to introduce you to during the course of your stay here."

"I should be delighted." She gazed into his face earnestly. "Richard, I do apologise if I offended you by dancing with Lord Hugh first." She licked her lips, a nervous expression knitting her brows together. "I could not very well deny him or tell him I was to dance with you when you were absent, could I?"

"My dear cousin, you are so amiable and easy-going that I doubt you could deny anyone a dance." He lightly touched her hand. "I am not offended by your not dancing with me," he whispered.

He watched her shoulders tilt downwards and relax.

"Now, if you wouldn't mind accompanying me, there are two more friends of mine that I'd like to make your acquaintance."

One quick nod was all he needed to offer her his arm and lead her away to where his friends were playing cards.

They entered the room, which was cooler but still packed with ladies and gentlemen all enjoying a break from dancing to play at the tables. The air was thick with cigar and pipe smoke. Richard squinted through the cloud to spy his friends beside an open window. "There," he pointed and negotiated their way around the tables.

Both George and Louis ended their game when they saw Georgiana on Richard's arm. He was pleased. Either of them would be a far better match for Georgiana than the lecherous Lord Hugh DeVere. He stepped back to allow them to talk after making the introductions, surprised at the sickening feeling in his stomach. He did not want any of them to marry his cousin.

Eight

After breakfast the next day, Georgiana had just settled herself down to make more decorations for the little tree in the dining room when the doorbell rang and a flurry of visitors began to call on them.

First of all came Richard's friends, Alexander Salisbury, Louis Ashton, and George Branford. Georgiana recoiled from the latter, who, in her opinion, had already had a skinful of wine that morning. *Or perhaps he has not recovered sufficiently from the night before,* she supposed.

After their arrival and the call for tea, the bell rang again and in trotted Lady Francesca with her brother, Hugh. Georgiana instantly felt her colour rise and averted her eyes from his. They brought with them a new acquaintance, Mrs

Nicolette Fotheringhay, who, Georgiana was delighted to discover, was the sister of Louis Ashton.

Georgiana's curiosity about the siblings was more than satisfied as Mrs Fotheringhay supplied them with such a long and fully detailed explanation of their family history, that she wanted nothing more than to flee the room after twenty minutes had elapsed. They lamented the French Revolution which caused their mother to escape the country to Britain and afterwards marry an Englishman and politician, the Right Honourable Ralph Ashton.

Georgiana frowned. "Surely her escape was fortuitous. Without it, she most likely would have been executed and neither yourself nor your brother would be here," pointing out the obvious.

Louis Ashton let out a bellowing guffaw from where he sat beside the window overlooking the street. "Well said, Miss Darcy. Well said! I tell Mama and Nicolette that all the time, but they always look on the dark side. They're such pessimists."

"Do not forget what Mama has suffered," Nicolette snapped.

Georgiana stood and handed round the plate of delicious Eccles cakes. Her chest roiled with emotions. She fought the irritation of such irrationality in Mrs Fotheringhay. "That is in the past now. Your dear mama has a good life now, safe here on these shores." She smiled into Mrs Fotheringhay's face, watching her jaw drop open at the comment. "Eccles cake? They're delicious. Cook is from Lancashire, and this is a delicacy from her hometown. In fact," Georgiana continued, ignoring Mrs Fotheringhay's discomfort, "they're awfully similar to mince pies, which Cook also makes exceedingly well indeed."

Mrs Fotheringhay mutely took one and a proffered plate.

"Fotheringhay...Fotheringhay..." Aunt Henrietta tapped her chin. "The name rings a bell. Is there not a Fotheringhay in the House of Lords?"

Georgiana continued to pass out the Eccles cakes and her eyes sparkled as she listened, entranced and in awe of her aunt's skill. How easily she cajoled the information out of Mrs Fotheringhay.

"Indeed, he is my husband," came the terse reply.

Georgiana almost dropped the plates in her hands. *Surely, Lord Fotheringhay is older than her father!*

"Oh, how splendid of your papa to have made you such a fortuitous match, my dear."

Catching Richard's eye fleetingly, Georgiana knew they were the only ones in the room who caught the mockery dripping from Aunt Henrietta's comment.

"Yes," Mrs Fotheringhay replied, lowering her eyes and picking at the sugar on top of the pastry.

"How marvellous! I suspect he is desirous of having an heir, is he not?"

Georgiana's mouth fell open and she caught herself just in time as she handed her aunt a plate with a pastry on it. She glared at the older woman who, having her face hidden from the company by Georgiana's body, winked at her niece.

Mrs Fotheringhay stuttered but could not give a response.

"Of course he is!" Aunt Henrietta declared. "All married men of good fortune are. And from what I hear, his fortune surpasses good."

Georgiana knew her aunt was having sport at the lady's expense. She did not like pessimistic attitudes either, but she was astounded at how an older person could get away with being so blunt. Picking up a pastry, Georgiana focussed her attention on not getting the crumbs all over herself—anything to not look at her aunt's smooth smile or Mrs Fotheringhay's aghast expression.

Thankfully, it seemed that Aunt Henrietta had had enough fun and she steered the conversation towards the delights of London—the ballet, opera, and theatre.

"Oh, my dear Lady Matlock," Lady Francesca's face lit up at the subject. "There are so many new plays and diversions this year. I do not know where to begin!" She rearranged the hem of her dress around her ankles, drawing the attention of the gentlemen.

Georgiana bit her tongue at the obvious flirtation and asked, "Where do you have your dresses made, Lady Francesca? I declare I have never seen so many shades of lavender before."

Again, another of Lady Francesca's favourite subjects. "Oh, my dear. It was obvious to me from the first moment that I laid eyes on you that an education in fashion was needed."

Georgiana remembered why she took an instant disliking to the lady. Her eyes narrowed.

"Fear not, my dear friend. I shall show you all the best houses in London."

Her smile was enough to make Georgiana's mouth run dry. She felt like a mouse caught in a cat's claw. "How very kind," she whimpered.

"Enough of fashion," Hugh DeVere chimed in. "I believe Miss Darcy would look well in anything she chose to wear!"

"Hugh!" Lady Francesca protested.

He cut her off. "I believe Lady Matlock asked about diversions." He stepped into the middle of the room and, with all eyes upon him, withdrew something from his inside pocket. "I have here in my hands six tickets to the ballet tonight." He caught Georgiana's eyes. "I hope you, your aunt, and your cousin will accompany me."

She opened her mouth to respond to his request when Lady Francesca cut across her.

"Six! Then for whom is the other? For I presume one is for me, Hugh!" Her voice took on a grating, shrill tone.

Hugh looked heavenward but did not turn around. "Of course one is for you, sister."

"Then, pray tell, for whom is the other?" Her voice cut the silence which descended like a knife.

Georgiana watched Hugh close his eyes, his feet firmly planted on the floor.

"I assumed we could invite someone else to join us. One of Colonel Fitzwilliam's friends or one of yours perhaps?" His jaw clenched.

In that instant, Georgiana realised Hugh was not quite as fond of his meddling sister as she had given them to believe. Her opinion of Hugh increased.

When he finally opened his eyes and gazed intently into hers, they shone with the same brilliance they had on the night she met him.

"Will you accept my invitation?" he asked, ignoring his sister, who continued to whine behind him.

With the smallest of looks at her aunt for permission, Georgiana said, "I would be delighted to accompany you, Lord Hugh."

She felt the burn of her cheeks as Richard stepped towards the still complaining lady. "I would be delighted to accompany you, Lady Francesca, to the ballet."

With one simple sentence, Richard silenced her. The angry red that suffused her face, melted away to be replaced by the bonnie and glowing red of a deep blush.

Georgiana's lips curled upwards and she had to hide her face. *She is sweet on Cousin Richard!*

Mentally, she made a list of the invitees. Aunt Henrietta, of course, herself and Lord Hugh made three. Richard and Lady Francesca made five.

"Mrs Fotheringhay are you available tonight for the ballet?" Hugh asked, finally turning around.

The poor woman was flustered and fiddled with her reticule. "I thank you for the invitation, Lord Hugh." She giggled and glanced away. "However, my husband and I are invited to dine with the Prime Minister tonight."

"Oh! Robert Banks Jenkinson...lucky you!" One or two of the men whistled.

"The Earl of Liverpool always puts on a grand dinner," Aunt Henrietta added, full of admiration. "I remember when I and my late husband, God rest his soul, were invited to dine with his own late father, Charles."

"I am certain you will have a wonderful evening," Hugh concluded.

From the expression Mrs Fotheringhay wore, Georgiana doubted that a wonderful evening was what the lady expected to have. She saw the jealousy reflected in her eyes and wondered what life with Lord Fotheringhay was truly like.

Louis cleared his throat. "Then, if I may be so bold." He tore himself away from propping up the mantelpiece and stood before them. "Might I present myself as the perfect addition to the party this evening?" He looked at them all in turn. "Three ladies and three gentlemen." He grinned engagingly, his eyes resting on Georgiana's face and tracing the line of her mouth.

She swallowed and shifted in her seat so that she was partly obscured behind Hugh. Overcome with nerves, she asked herself why a man looking at her so appreciatively would make her feel so uncomfortable.

"We shall be ever such a happy bunch!" he declared, his grin deepening.

Georgiana bristled from the suspicion that he was enjoying her discomfort.

Nine

If Georgiana thought that the ballroom was noisy, she could barely stand the cacophony of sound in the foyer of the theatre that night. She took deep steadying breaths and resisted the desire to place her gloved hands over her ears.

The decision on what to wear was agony. She laid out all her dresses on the bed and, with Meg's help, she chose the best one. Lady Francesca's words echoed in her head like a judgement. Never before had Georgiana Darcy felt inadequate or inferior to anyone, but Lady Francesca had the ability to make her shrink into insignificance with simply one sentence. She puffed up the sleeves on her dress.

"You look perfect," Richard leant in close and whispered in her ear. "Do not be so fastidious. You are far superior to many of the ladies here."

"Richard," she sighed. "That is not what I want. You know I abhor such pride as that."

"Then what is it?"

She held her breath as he scanned her face, knowing full well that she could not erase the worried expression she wore. "Lady Francesca."

"Oh," Richard replied, grimacing. "I wonder if she would have a pleasant word to say about any of the dresses that Queen Charlotte herself wears."

Georgiana cocked her head to the side. "I believe you may be right, but I cannot push out her voice from my mind."

"Then, cousin," Richard cooed soothingly, taking hold of her hands and gazing deeply into her eyes, "let mine drown hers out entirely. You look beautiful tonight. Your dress suits you well."

Georgiana saw only sincerity in his countenance. She arched her shoulders and felt the tension leave them, knowing her cousin spoke from his heart. "I apologise, Richard."

He shook his head, half-closing his eyes. "There is no need to apologise. Sometimes people say things that should be only taken with a pinch of salt. You do not have to live up to anyone's expectations but your own."

"How is it you always know the perfect thing to say to me?" She leant onto his arm.

"Because I know you only too well. Neither of us was brought up to spend all our time pandering to the whims of society. I believe our parents have done us a great service in that."

Glancing around the extravagantly decorated foyer, she giggled. "I believe you are right there."

"So do not attempt to conform now you are here. Enjoy yourself, Georgiana. In a month or so, you will be going back to Derbyshire and sanity."

Richard's wry smile and deep-throated chuckle set off her giggles again.

"Shall we take our seats?" Hugh interrupted their tête-a-tête. His eyes bored into Georgiana's, and she felt their meaning intensely. He held out his arm for her to take.

She stole a brief glance at Richard's expression and could not read it. He watched Hugh carefully. His eyes that a second before had been so filled with mirth were now as cold as steel.

Georgiana recognised they were the invitees, and she felt it would be rude to refuse Hugh's proffered arm. Fixing a smile on her face, she inclined her head and accepted his arm.

"I hope the ballet is to your liking, Miss Darcy," he drawled.

Georgiana caught the look of triumph in Hugh's eyes, directed at Richard, as she relinquished her hold on her cousin. Almost imperceptibly, she stiffened. *What is that all about?*

The passages and hallways of the theatre were thronged with people. Georgiana could not tell where they were heading, but Hugh seemed to know his way as he navigated a path towards the staircase that led to the boxes on one side of the stage. Ladies and gentlemen passed them on both sides, and Georgiana was certain that, if she had not had such a sure grip on Hugh's arm, she would have lost her footing on the plush deep red carpeting.

He covered her hand with his own, and an electric jolt shot deep into her stomach, causing her breathing to falter.

The box, once they'd fought their way to it, was furnished to seat their entire party. Hugh made certain they were the first to arrive. He chose the centre front seats for himself and Georgiana. She could not have dreamt of a better situation to see the stage so well.

"Are you comfortable, Miss Darcy?" Hugh asked, just as the others began to join them.

She was touched by his attention. "Yes, thank you. I am."

Georgiana watched in fascination as the theatre filled up and the other patrons took their seats. She sensed someone sit down next to her and was relieved to see it was Richard and beside him, Lady Francesca. On Hugh's other side sat Aunt Henrietta, and lastly Louis Ashton. The seats were slightly staggered, allowing all six of them to be on the front row and permitting them all the best possible view of the performance.

Georgiana sat back and listened contentedly to Aunt Henrietta and Louis gossiping about society, occasionally punctuated by Lady Francesca doing her best to engage Richard in a deeper conversation. She was surprised he was not being his usual convivial self. However, she was not oblivious to the tension between him and Hugh. Not for the first time, she wondered if they had known each other longer than she believed.

Georgiana was overjoyed as the candles were snuffed and the curtain rose. She was held spellbound throughout the entire performance, entranced by the grace, strength, and beauty of the dancers.

When the curtain fell again for the intermission and the candles were relit, Georgiana almost cried out in protest. She had no wish for refreshment. She wanted the dancers to captivate her once more. She struggled to remain polite as Hugh asked her if she wished to take a glass of wine with him.

Turning her face, Georgiana wrestled with her facial muscles, willing them into a friendly smile. "That would be lovely. Thank you, Hugh," she lied.

As Hugh bowed and left the box with the other gentlemen to fetch refreshments, Georgiana stood to stretch out her legs, not realising how stiff they'd become.

"Well, what do you think, my dear?" Aunt Henrietta asked her from her end of the box.

"I like it ever so much, Aunt." Her eyes shone with delight.

Aunt Henrietta chuckled, and Georgiana drew closer.

"That's not what I meant," she whispered, her eyes full of laughter.

Georgiana perched on the edge of the seat. "What did you mean?"

"I meant," Aunt Henrietta lowered her voice even more as she peeked over her niece's shoulder to see if Lady Francesca was looking.

Georgiana involuntarily also looked. Lady Francesca was waving at her acquaintances down in the stalls.

"I meant what do you think of your overly attentive chaperone, Lord Hugh?" Her eyes widened, pressing home her meaning.

"Oh," Georgiana replied, just stopping herself from gasping loudly. She stole another glance at Lady Francesca. Relieved they were not overheard, she turned back to her aunt. "There is nothing to dislike, Aunt. He is amiable and attentive."

Aunt Henrietta smiled indulgently. "But what do you think of him?"

Georgiana's brows met. "I don't follow you."

"Personally," Aunt Henrietta sighed. "Do you think him amiable and handsome enough to fall in love with?"

Georgiana was speechless and sat staring agog at her aunt.

The older woman raised her eyebrows in enquiry. "Well? Do you?"

No matter how hard she tried to answer her aunt, Georgiana's mouth simply opened and closed.

"Your impression of a trout is admirable, my dear." Aunt Henrietta covered her mouth with a gloved hand as she laughed. "However, a simple yes or no will suffice."

Georgiana gripped her reticule tighter, finally gaining control of her faculties. "I admit he is very handsome, but

Aunt," again she stole a glance at Lady Francesca, "I have not thought of matrimony at all regarding him."

Aunt Henrietta sat back in the chair, a look of complete satisfaction written on her face. "As it should be, my dear." She held up a finger. "Never be in a hurry to marry. Especially not before you know the real character of the man you have fallen in love with or set your sights upon."

"Excellent advice!"

The pair of women looked up in surprise to discover Lady Francesca standing beside them.

"Lady Francesca! How good of you to come over and join us."

Georgiana stared mindlessly as Aunt Henrietta recovered her wits first.

"I could not very well miss out on such an interesting conversation, could I, Lady Matlock?" She beamed. "I must say that I agree wholeheartedly with your advice." She lowered her voice conspiratorially, despite them being the only ones left in the box. "There are far too many cads in society willing to prey upon the first rich young lady to cross their paths. One cannot be too careful." She gazed pointedly at Georgiana.

"Precisely what we were saying," Aunt Henrietta replied for her.

Lady Francesca straightened up, a look of mischief playing on her face. "And which gentleman in particular were you discussing?"

Georgiana paled. She could feel the blood draining from her face. The last thing she wanted was to plant the seed of suspicion that she preferred Lord Hugh.

"No one gentleman in particular, my dear."

Georgiana tilted her head to the side. "We were speaking generally, of course."

"Of course," Lady Francesca continued to grin. "I will be the soul of discretion."

Opening her mouth to protest, Georgiana's utterance was cut short by the reappearance of the gentlemen.

"Here we are, ladies!" Hugh declared, handing Georgiana a glass of red wine. "I hope we haven't missed out on any juicy gossiping." He winked at his sister.

"Oh, Hugh!" Lady Francesca giggled. "You know it would be imprudent for us to tell tales, especially about the very gentlemen we were discussing."

Again, Georgiana felt the blood drain from her face and her stomach pitched downwards.

"Indeed?" Hugh grinned like a cat that had been given cream as he re-seated himself.

"Lady Francesca jests with you," Georgiana snapped, standing, and returning to her chair. She placed the glass back on the tray on the corner table as she passed, the wine untouched.

"Do not be offended, Miss Darcy." Hugh smirked with satisfaction as he spoke. "It is no crime to talk about young men. I believe all women do it."

"Quite right too!" Lady Francesca slipped into her seat, shifting it a little closer to Richard. "After all, if we did not, we would not know with whom we were in competition for the gentleman's affections."

Georgiana stared in front of her, her eyes unseeing. She bristled at the insinuation that they were discussing which of the men they preferred. She was beginning to wish she could go home.

"Lady Francesca," Aunt Henrietta spoke up, loudly enough to be heard at the other end of the box. "It is unkind to jest so and lead your brother to believe we discussed that which we did not."

Georgiana did not look back, but she could feel the change in atmosphere.

"I beg your forgiveness, Lady Matlock, but that was not my understanding of the discussion you were having with your niece. But..." Georgiana heard Lady Francesca's fan snap open "...my lips will be sealed on the subject, especially to save dear Miss Darcy's blushes."

Once more she made the insinuation even after Aunt Henrietta had refuted her claim. Georgiana silently fumed. Her nails dug so deeply into her silk reticule that she was convinced she will have ruined it. She cared not. She could feel all eyes on her, and she fought the tears that stung her eyes. She hated the idea that Richard would now believe she was falling in love with Lord Hugh.

"Come now, Miss Darcy," Hugh nudged her as the candles were snuffed again. "Do not be offended. I am flattered you think so well of me."

A spiteful retort died on her tongue as the last of the candles sputtered and died and the curtain rose once more to the raucous accompaniment of the orchestra in the pit.

* * *

Richard watched his young cousin squirm with discomfort once they returned to the box with the glasses of wine. He disliked the direction the conversation was heading but felt his mother dealt with it sufficiently.

He was, however, stunned to hear Lady Francesca so openly continue the conversation.

He kept his mouth shut and his eye on his cousin. She wasn't happy. She sat bolt upright in the chair and her back was stiff. He watched her jaw stiffen and clench. He could not read her expression from the side, but having known her since she was born, he was pretty confident he could read her body language. She was angry and more than a little upset.

Does she prefer Lord Hugh above any other after so short an acquaintance? The very thought left him bereft.

"Are you quite well, Colonel?" Lady Francesca purred in his ear as the music began to play once more.

"Quite well, thank you," he replied shortly and returned his face to the stage, although his eyes flicked repeatedly to Georgiana. *Oh, how I wish I could whisk you away from here and take you home,* he lamented, feeling guilty after promising to protect her from harm. *How can one protect a lady from gossip and careless tongue-wagging?*

The remainder of the ballet passed in an interminable blur for Richard. He was consumed with the overwhelming sensation of having let both his cousins down.

As they stood to leave, he could almost hear Darcy laugh. *"You cannot put a stop to people's tongues, Richard. That is the one thing that most people in society have the least control over."*

He knew Darcy was right. The only thing he could hope for was the opportunity to speak with Georgiana himself, either on the journey home or when they arrived back.

His stomach clenched. He needed to know if she was falling in love with Lord Hugh DeVere.

Thankfully, the ballet came to an end and they filtered with everyone else, bustling for the exit. Lady Francesca tightly held on to his arm. He glanced down at her and saw her look up at him with her eyes wide and full of admiration.

Oh, dear God, he groaned inside. *Please tell me she has not set her sights on me.* He baulked at the thought of spending his days attached to such a gossipy, sanctimonious harridan as she. All the same, he mustered a kindly smile to bestow upon her. "Never fear. We shall make it out of here in one piece," he quipped.

Richard was grateful that they travelled back to Pembroke Square in their own carriage.

He watched, impressed, as his mother and Georgiana both eloquently and graciously thanked the DeVeres for such a wonderful evening of entertainment.

He tensed as Lord Hugh kissed the back of Georgiana's hand. He was grateful it remained gloved and shielded her skin from his lips.

Richard watched on as Lord Hugh held on to her hand far longer than was necessary and looked deeply into her eyes. "Until we meet again tomorrow, Miss Darcy. I shall not rest until I am by your side once more."

It was all Richard could do to prevent himself from tearing DeVere away from his fair cousin and bodily shoving him into his own carriage.

He was gratified to see Lord Hugh's words had no positive effect on his cousin. Her reply caused him to turn aside, hiding the laugh that was on the verge of bursting out.

"Thank you for your kind attention, Lord Hugh, but I fear we shall not be home to visitors tomorrow. I believe with such a late night, we shall attend to family matters."

Turning back, Richard caught the blatant pout on Lord Hugh's face. "You would wound a gentleman so?"

Richard was instantly by his cousin's side. "Miss Darcy is correct. My mother is an elderly widow, Lord Hugh. We shall rest tomorrow."

He handed Georgiana into the carriage before Lord Hugh could utter another word.

Richard was too well brought up as to leave it there. He looked back at the brother and sister. "Again, we thank you for the evening's entertainment." He smiled. "I am sure I speak for the ladies when I say we hope to repeat this." He purposely did not add when or soon. He then addressed his friend. "Louis, are you coming with us or with the DeVeres?"

Out of the corner of his eye, he watched Lady Francesca's mouth fall open.

"I...I've been invited back to the DeVeres for a cup or two." Louis Ashton looked Lady Francesca up and down as he spoke and sank in Richard's estimation.

What is it about women that can turn men into monsters? he asked himself. "Very well. I hope you all have a pleasant time." He reached out and took Lady Francesca's hand, kissing it lightly. "Lady Francesca, it was a pleasure."

"The pleasure was all mine, Colonel," she gushed.

He bowed and climbed into the carriage.

All three of them smiled and waved as they pulled away into the night.

Georgiana leant across the carriage, lightly touching his knee. "Thank you," she whispered.

His heart swelled within him. That was all he needed to hear for his emotions to settle back down.

"Yes. Thank you, Richard."

He glanced over at his mother. She was tight-lipped.

"I don't mind saying I like Lord Hugh, but his sister!" she burst out.

Laughter ripped through the carriage.

"And I do not particularly like being called elderly, Richard!" she snapped.

"I apologise, Mama. It was for a good cause."

"I know." His mother reached out and took hold of Georgiana's hand. "My dear, if you wish to see Lady Francesca again, and it is none of my business if you do so socially or not, then please do not include me in any of the arrangements. I do not think I could maintain my countenance if I had to endure that woman again for an entire evening without a means of escape."

Again their laughter roared aloud.

"I promise, Aunt," Georgiana replied when she had stopped laughing.

I do not wish you to see them ever again, whether socially again or not, Richard thought.

Ten

Georgiana stayed up writing her thoughts down in her journal. She wasn't too regular at writing in it, but whenever she felt conflicted, she believed it helped. She then wrote a letter to Elizabeth and, yawning, turned in for the night.

She awoke late and joined her aunt in the breakfast room for coffee.

Aunt Henrietta smiled, looking tired as she sat down. "Good morning, my dear. I see you are as tired by last night as I am." She passed the coffeepot. "It is still hot."

"I confess I stayed up late writing to Elizabeth," Georgiana replied, pouring herself a cup of the steaming liquid and savouring its strong scent.

"Yes. I saw it in the hall, ready to go to the post." Aunt Henrietta stifled a yawn. "I am convinced my days of gallivanting around town are long past. I believe it will take me a day or two to recover from such a late night."

"Not to worry, Aunt. We shall remain at home tonight. I brought a book or two I would like to read, upon Elizabeth's recommendation."

Aunt Henrietta looked up sharply, her attention piqued. "Really? Oh, do share them with me when you've finished. Elizabeth is always such a good judge of books."

"Yes, she is," Georgiana smiled into her coffee cup and watched her aunt read from a piece of paper laid on the yellow tablecloth. "What is it, Aunt?"

The older woman huffed and rubbed her face. "Nothing to concern yourself with, just household expenses." She nodded towards Georgiana's coffee cup. "It seems the import levies for coffee are increasing, as are those for candles." She shook her head from side to side. "Oh, if only our fathers and mothers taught us well how to manage household accounts without a husband."

"Will Richard not see to it?" she asked, concerned at how drained her aunt looked. "Shall I fetch him?"

"Yes, please do" came the weary reply.

Georgiana was out of her chair before Aunt Henrietta had finished speaking, she was so concerned over her health. She ran up the stairs and to Richard's room. The pair almost collided as he exited at the same time.

With shortness of breath, Georgiana explained the situation as they descended the stairs together. "I am convinced her fatigue is not entirely owing to being out late last night. I fear the running of the home weighs heavily upon her without Uncle Thomas."

Richard merely nodded once and squeezed her hand. "Thank you, Georgiana. I shall take care of it."

She stood in the hallway watching helplessly as he strode into the breakfast room and straight up to his mother. Georgiana thought it best to give them a moment or two alone. She dallied by the hall table and was gratified to see the letter plate was empty; her missive to Elizabeth was on its way to Hertfordshire.

Slowly returning to her late breakfast, Georgiana looked on, her heart touched by the tender display of affection between mother and son. Richard embraced Aunt Henrietta and held her tight while she wept.

Upon hearing the sound, Georgiana turned away.

"No, dearest child. Come back," Aunt Henrietta called out, her voice cracking with emotion. "You are family, my dear."

Richard held out his hand to her, and Georgiana tiptoed back into the room.

"Forgive me," Aunt Henrietta wept. "I still am overcome from time to time."

"You have nothing to apologise for, Aunt." She took Richard's hand and knelt on the parquet flooring before Aunt Henrietta. "I would think there was something amiss if you weren't overcome now and then." Georgiana pecked her on the cheek.

"I ought to have stepped in before, Mama." Richard smoothed the shawl on her shoulders. "I will be more than happy to do all I can."

"You are a good son." Aunt Henrietta turned her head and wept into his waistcoat.

Georgiana looked up into his face and saw such deep love there that she too was moved to tears. "Do you wish to remain here in London for the season, Aunt?"

Aunt Henrietta sat up straight and dabbed at her face with a napkin. "Of course, I do." She cleared her throat. "We came her for the diversion, didn't we?"

"Well, yes, but I do not mind in the least if you are not diverted and wish to travel into Hertfordshire and stay with the Bingleys at Netherfield Park for Christmas." Georgiana searched her aunt's eyes for any hint that she wanted to leave.

"No, my dear. I became disturbed over the household accounts and nothing more. It is at times like these that I need him the most."

Georgiana's brows knit together. "I can only imagine."

"But we are here to enjoy ourselves, and you will not enjoy the company of a certain young gentleman if we retire to Hertfordshire."

"Aunt..." Georgiana sputtered, furious with herself for blushing at the mere mention of Lord Hugh.

"I shall be fine. I assure you. Let us fix our gaze on your happiness now." She patted Richard and Georgiana on the hands. "Come along. The coffee will be getting cold."

They joined her at the table, eating scones with their coffee. Georgiana was concerned about her aunt, but having Richard by her side appeared to have lifted a great weight from about his mother's shoulders. Her face seemed less lined and filled with worry, her smile less forced.

"Have the DeVeres sent word?" Richard asked, and Georgiana caught the hard edge to his voice.

"No, I do not believe so," his mother replied.

"Good," he replied, buttering a scone.

"No, no, no!" Aunt Henrietta waved a warning finger in the air. "I do not believe it is good. Perhaps we were a little too hasty last night."

Both Richard and Georgiana stared at her.

"How so?" he asked, a scone held in mid-air.

"They were very kind in procuring tickets for the ballet and, just because we are not so fond of their manners, we ought not slight them."

Georgiana watched as Richard carefully replaced the scone on the china plate. "What do you suggest, Mama?"

"I was thinking," she began, taking a large daub of quince jam on her knife, "of having them over for dinner."

"Here?"

Richard's face was such a comical picture of incredulity, that Georgiana could barely contain the giggle that rose up inside her.

"Yes, here," Aunt Henrietta glared at Richard. "Just a little get-together. A thank-you, if you will. Then our obligations are fulfilled."

"Right." Richard stared down at his scone as though it were unfamiliar to him.

"Then we can see if Lord Hugh truly is the right beau to court our dear Georgiana."

Her mouth falling open, Georgiana choked on her words. "Court me?"

"Now, Mother. I think—"

"Fie, Richard! Who cares what you think when our little Georgiana is falling in love!" She bit into her scone and chewed while Richard and Georgiana gaped at her. "Oh, matchmaking is such fun! The son of a duke as well!"

Eleven

Richard had to get out of the house. He hurriedly ate a scone and downed a lukewarm cup of coffee, then, after speaking to the housekeeper and butler about the accounts, departed the house in a rush.

He was in such haste, he forgot his gloves and scarf. Cursing himself in frustration, he hailed a hackney cab. He knew where he would go—straight to Alexander Salisbury's home.

His friend was not surprised to see him. "How fared the ballet last night?" he laughed as he led Richard into his study.

"Is it too early?" he asked, clinking a crystal whisky tumbler against a decanter on a stand in the corner.

"Not today it isn't, Alex," Richard replied, slumping down in an overstuffed chair by the window. "Is it me or is it colder?"

"No, it's definitely colder. I've ordered more coal." Alex handed Richard a generous glass of whisky and sat down opposite him, his legs crossed. "So, let it out. What's got you so twisted up?"

Richard stared into the fire for a moment, gathering his thoughts. "What do you know of Lord Hugh DeVere?"

Alex snorted. "In or out of genteel society?" he cocked his head sideways and lifted his brows.

"All of it." Richard's forehead settled into a scowl. "Is he the same man of whom I've heard tell?"

"Hmm...that all depends on what you've heard told."

"Alex..." Richard warned.

His friend held his hands up in defence. "Very well. I know him well from the gentleman's club, where I wouldn't advise anyone to play cards with him, if you know what I mean."

"He's good? He cheats?" Richard prompted.

"Possibly both," he replied pulling a cigar from his pocket, snipping the end off, and lighting it. "There has been some talk of card-counting."

Richard swirled the whisky in the glass, breathed in the intoxicating vapour, and gulped down a mouthful. "Hardly unusual. What else?"

Alex took his time in responding, dragging deeply on the cigar, holding his breath, and then blowing out smoke rings.

Richard watched them slowly float towards the ceiling and evaporate.

"You know about the recent scandal, of course."

Richard's attention snapped back to his friend. "Scandal?"

"You mean you haven't heard?" Alex sat forward, the cheekiest grin on his lips. "Such a juicy morsel it is too."

Richard groaned, unsure whether he had to stomach to hear it or not.

"Isn't he the lucky one who was dancing with your delectable cousin the other night?" Alex taunted.

Richard's scowl deepened. "Yes." He glowered at his friend, willing him to speak. Inside, he was in a murderous turmoil. He didn't even know what the juicy gossip was, but he fought the desire to throttle the man all the same.

Alex sucked the air in through his teeth. "Now I can see the reason for your foul mood, my friend."

"I promised both her and her cousin—"

"Fitzwilliam Darcy?"

"Indeed." Richard breathed out heavily. "I promised them both I would take good care of her and make certain she did not run into trouble."

Alex stuck out his chin. "Is she the kind of girl to get into trouble?"

"No!" Richard clenched his jaw when he heard his friend chuckle at him. "You know what I mean. This is her first season in society."

"Right." Alex nodded sharply. "Well, then," he dragged long and hard on his cigar again "you need to be armed with all the facts." He blew the smoke out, surrounding his head with a thick blue cloud. "Or at least what everyone seems to be chattering on about him anyway."

"I do." Richard drained his glass, stood up, and helped himself to another drink. Alex held out his glass and Richard sloshed more whisky into it too.

Once he sat back down, Alex began to tell everything he knew. Richard sat enthralled and disgusted at the same time.

"And so Miss Margaret Ainsworth and Lord Hugh's little by-blow are left high and dry."

"Has he no morals?" Richard growled.

"Oh," Alex coughed on the smoke, "apparently his father, the Duke, found out about the dalliance and has come down hard on him."

Richard's stomach tightened. "What?" His mouth opened and closed.

"Margaret is of little consequence," Alex explained, gesturing. "As the third son of a duke, Lord Hugh must marry a fortune or be left penniless when his old man shuffles off this mortal coil."

Richard stared into nothingness. The words *Margaret is of little consequence* reverberated around his skull. "What of the infant?"

"What of it?"

The words stuck in Richard's throat.

"You can't go around rescuing the entire world, Richard." Alex scoffed. "I know you've become some sort of hero on the Iberian Peninsula, but..."

"The child..." Richard managed.

"A boy, if you must know." Alex huffed, drank a little and smoked his cigar, studying Richard. "Margaret had a little boy. She named him Walter, after her father."

Richard sat up straight. "Where are they now?"

"What? You're not thinking..."

"Where are they now?"

One infuriated look was all that was needed to have Alex spurting out the information Richard desired. "Her father has taken her to the coast. Bournemouth, I think."

Richard finished the last drop of whisky and stood. "How can I find them?"

"You're serious, aren't you?" Alex's mouth fell open as he also stood.

"How can I find them?"

"Rumours have it the father has made her take a new name. I doubt you'll find them."

Richard cocked a brow. "Has the infant been baptised?"

"Not that I know of." Alex stood, looking deflated. "This is so important to you?"

"I need to know if this is the truth or just idle gossip whose aim is to destroy the man." He rounded on his friend. "My mother is bent on matching Miss Darcy and Lord Hugh." He swallowed down the bile that rose to his throat. "And from what I can see, she is already partial to him."

Slowly, Alex stubbed out the cigar in a brass ashtray. "Do you want company?"

For the first time in hours, Richard smiled.

* * *

Georgiana had never seen such a fuss. Richard was in a hurry, stating he had urgent business in the south of England, and Aunt Henrietta was beside herself, crying that she thought Richard was running away from them both.

"Mother!" he tried to calm her nerves. "There is no time to lose. Alexander and I must leave immediately."

"But why?" she protested. "You have not furnished me with a sufficient explanation, Richard. And what about the dinner party? We can't very well have it without you here."

"Then wait until I return. I shan't be long." He kissed her forehead. "And do not fret, Mama."

His horse, along with Alex's, had been brought around to the house and awaited their riders on the street.

Georgiana accompanied her aunt to the top step. She watched as the stable boy held the heads of the horses while Richard strapped on his bag.

"I promise to return within two days. I know what I have to do and where I have to go."

"Won't you even tell your mother?" Aunt Henrietta whined, gripping Georgiana's hand painfully.

"Mama, I cannot let you know every aspect of my business," Richard replied, his temper clearly running out. "The quicker I depart, the quicker I may return." He ran back up the steps and kissed his mother's cheek. "Set the dinner party for Wednesday night, and I promise to be there, by hook or by crook."

Aunt Henrietta began to weep.

Georgiana stepped forward. "Ride well and stay safe. Your mother needs you to return in one piece."

She watched Richard's expression soften as he gazed upon her. "And you?"

"Me?" Georgiana's brow knit in confusion.

"Do you need me to return in one piece?" he asked quietly.

She felt her cheeks burn again. *Why do I blush like a child when a man speaks thus to me?* "I would dearly like you to return in one piece." Puzzled, she believed Richard to be holding his breath. "And safe."

He smiled brightly enough for her to feel its warmth.

"And quickly, please," she breathed, surprised at her own desire to have him return.

He took hold of her free hand and kissed the back of it. "I shall."

Georgiana watched, her heart thumping in her chest, as he bounded down the steps, mounted his horse and, within a few seconds, was gone, leaving the two women standing futilely staring into the street.

Twelve

ichard knew he was driving his horse too hard. A voice in the back of his mind warned him to ease up or risk injuring the poor beast.

They left London behind long ago and galloped their way along the rough southwesterly road. As a village loomed on the horizon, Richard reined in his horse. He was painfully aware of how much the animal was perspiring and needed rest. As did he, his stomach growled and reminded him of his meagre breakfast, and they stopped at an inn and took a meal.

The meat pie, ale, bread and cheese refreshed them; but when they got back outside, it was clear the horses were not.

Richard looked around him and sought out the livery stables where they hired two fine mares, leaving their own to be taken care of.

Once they were back on the road towards Bournemouth, Richard rode like man possessed. Alex, who had lived most of his life in and around cities, was not the horseman Richard was and had a difficult time keeping pace with him. Even so, by the time they reached Winchester with its imposing medieval cathedral, Richard had calmed himself sufficiently to slow down and allow his friend to ride by his side.

"Do you want to stop here?" he called out.

"Yes. I really think we ought to stop for the night, Richard. The sun is beginning to set, and the horses are tired."

Richard didn't need telling twice. He knew the value of keeping a horse well looked after and had been wracked with guilt over driving his own so hard when they first set out. Moreover, his fingers and toes were numb from the cold wind. He'd lost the feeling in his nose hours ago. "Very well. We'll stable these and procure two more. We'll find a tavern, get some hot food in our bellies and some sleep. But I want to set off again in the early hours. We have no time to lose."

Alex didn't say a word. He merely nodded in agreement.

Richard hoped his friend understood and did not think he'd lost his mind.

They found stables and lodgings easily enough. Very few people were travelling at this time of the year and in such inclement weather—even there in the south.

He almost groaned with delight when the innkeeper told them that dinner was stew with potatoes. It was just what they needed. The pair seated themselves before the inn's inglenook fireplace.

"What do you intend to do when we find her?" Alex asked, rubbing his hands before the fire.

Richard saw Alex's fingers were as red and painful as his own and wanted to apologise for putting his friend through this but remembered Alex had volunteered to come along. "I need to ask her if..." his eyes darted nervously towards the bar, he then lowered his voice "...if Lord Hugh is the babe's father."

"Of course," Alex replied, pulling off his boots and wincing in pain. "And then what?"

Richard sighed. He had not thought that far ahead. His main preoccupation had been to make sure that Georgiana was safe from a rake. She had already been in the path of Wickham. She didn't need to go through that again.

His heart went out to Margaret and her infant. Her reputation now lay in tatters, and he doubted very much whether any man would want to marry her now.

"Perhaps her father has had the wisdom to not only change her name but come up with a story."

"Hmm?"

"Well, perhaps...a widow." Alex shrugged.

Richard smiled sadly. "Yes, that would solve many problems all at once."

"I have heard of it being done. A lady's reputation is fragile and once lost it can never be recovered."

Richard studied his face. "You sound as though you speak from experience."

Alex puffed out his cheeks and rested his heels on the hearthstone. "A childhood chum got a girl with child and his father paid her family to move away, say she was widowed, and change her name."

"All that, rather than own up to what he did?" The whole scenario infuriated Richard.

"Indeed. She was the daughter of a baker. Not the kind of woman this fellow's father wanted for a daughter-in-law."

"I suppose that is how the Duke feels."

"No doubt."

"We have to find her," Richard replied feeling the injustice of it all keenly.

Alex stared into the cracking flames. "Agreed."

* * *

When they awoke, it was still dark outside. The innkeeper had kindly come, in his nightshirt, to rouse them from sleep—for an extra shilling. Richard and Alex dressed hastily in the chill air before dawn. Looking out of the window, Richard could see there was a sharp frost. His breath clouded in front of his face, steaming up the window. From his vantage point, he could see their horses being led out to the front of the building.

By the time they reached the bar, two flagons of ale and stale bread and cheese awaited them. Richard, knowing full well that he needed sustenance in such cold weather, tore two chunks of cheese and bread and handed them to Alex before biting into his own. The ale, chilled in the unheated bar, helped to wash down the hard bread.

Richard's eyes were heavy as he headed out the door and mounted the horse provided for him. He knew what he had to do that day. They had to reach the outskirts of Bournemouth and ask for Margaret Ainsworth and her family. Richard thanked his lucky stars that Bournemouth was not as big a city as London. A person could disappear entirely in London, whereas in Bournemouth it was likely the locals would be gossiping about the new family for years to come. Richard intended to use that to his advantage.

The pair rode on in silence until the first few dwellings came into view just after dawn. Fortune favoured them. The milkmaids were out in the fields milking the cows. Richard reined in his horse, stopping beside the five-bar gate. Alex followed suit.

Richard dismounted and, putting on his best and most charming smile, strode towards the gate. Immediately he caught the eye of more than one of the maids. "Good morning," he called out.

One of the maids, a buxom young girl with a ruddy complexion, stopped what she was doing and, rising, carried her milk pail towards them. "Morning," she responded eyeing them both up and down. "You be new around 'ere?"

Richard liked the sound of her accent, lilting, and songlike. "We are indeed. We are looking for some friends of ours who have recently moved here."

"Oh, aye," she replied lifting up the pail. "Could I offer youse gentlemans some milk?"

Alex step forward. “Yes, please.” He drank from the side of the pail while Richard conversed with her.

“Yes. They must have come here in the last week or so.” He leant nonchalantly on the gate. “I suspect that nothing happens around here without you knowing about it. Am I right?”

His question was answered by the rising colour in her cheeks. Richard thought she looked quite pretty when she blushed.

“I do keep my eyes open, if that’s what you means,” she replied, puffing up her already ample chest with pride.

Richard did his best not to look satisfied. “I wonder if you know them.”

“There be a new family just north of here. They buyed a ’ouse, so they did.” The corners of her mouth turned down and her eyes twinkled with unshed tears. “’Tis a sad tale an’ make no mistake. For she, the young missus, is widowed an’ with a babe in arms,” the milkmaid blurted out.

Alex choked on the milk.

Could this be them? “Oh, that is a sad tale indeed.” Richard mimicked her expression. “I wonder, did they tell you their name at all?” He inched closer towards her. “I only ask because I would not wish to upset an already grieving family with our arrival if they were not the family we are looking for.”

“I knew you was a kind ’un the minute I sawed you.” She grinned revealing some missing teeth.

“Thank you,” Richard bowed his head. “The family we are looking for are called the Ainsworths.”

The milkmaid's eyes opened wide. "I think that be them!" she almost shrieked.

"Wonderful!" Alex exclaimed, handing the pail back to her.

Her eyes narrowed. "How youse be knowing 'em?"

Richard was fast on the uptake. "We are acquaintances of the lady's late husband."

"Oh, really?"

Alex nodded. "Yes, really. We want to make sure that she is well taken care of and to pay our respects."

The maid dug the toe of her boot into the dirt. "That's mighty kind o' youse."

"Where precisely is this house they bought?" Richard pressed.

"No more'n three miles direct north," she pointed.

"Thank you," Richard beamed at her. "You have been most helpful, Miss..."

"People 'round 'ere jus' call me Maisie." Her blush returned deeper than before.

"Well, I am most grateful to you, Maisie." Richard pulled out a coin from his pocket and handed it to her, squeezing it tightly in her chubby fist. "Most grateful."

"You're welcome, sir." She chewed the inside of her cheek for a second before asking, "Might we be seein' youse 'round 'ere more often?"

"That, I cannot say." Richard straightened up and took a step back. "That all very much depends on whether the young lady is distressed by our visit or not."

Alex nodded beside him looking suitably sombre. “Yes, we would not wish to cause her any more distress than that which she is presently suffering.”

The maid laid her head to the side. “Oh, that’s so very thoughtful o’ youse.” She gazed back at Richard, tilting her head down, and peering at him from under her lashes. “I do so very much ’ope that youse will return, mister.”

Richard bowed and doffed his top hat. “I wish you a very good day, Maisie. Thank you for the information and the milk.” He treated her, one last time, to his most charming smile before remounting his horse.

As they rode off, Richard stole a quick glance back. Maisie remained at the gate watching them as they rode away. He waved.

Alex whistled. “I never took you for such a charmer, Richard.”

“Neither did I!” Richard burst out laughing.

No matter how amusing the situation was, they had the information they needed, or at least Richard hoped they had. There was a new family not far away from them now whose daughter was recently widowed with a young babe.

Silently, Richard prayed the young lady was Margaret Ainsworth. He knew the longer it took to find the young lady and her infant, the less hope they had of finding out if Lord Hugh DeVere was a scoundrel or if he was simply maligned.

Thirteen

Georgiana paced up and down the full width of the house in Pembroke Square, then she turned and paced from the back to the front. Ever since Richard's departure, she had felt unsettled and ill at ease, unable to think of anything else but him. For the umpteenth time, she resisted looking at the grandfather clock in the hallway.

"Knowing the time will not bring them back any quicker," she huffed.

The previous night had cleared the skies to reveal the majesty of the universe, but it had brought with it a heavy frost. Georgiana had watched as many who attempted their morning walk slipped and slid about on the icy pavements and cobblestone streets. Aunt Henrietta deemed it better to stay indoors, which only increased Georgiana's sense of agitation.

After lunch of Scotch broth, thick chunks of homemade bread, and more of Cook's delicious mince pies, both Georgiana and Aunt Henrietta were surprised to hear the doorbell ring.

Georgiana did not know whether to be elated or disappointed as she strode out into the hallway and stopped dead, her stomach sinking in disappointment, upon seeing who their visitors were—Lady Francesca and her brother Lord Hugh.

"Oh, my dear! It is good that you have not ventured outside," the former chirped as she untied her bonnet, handed her muff to Hobbs, and strode towards Georgiana. "The streets are in a terrible state." She forwent the courtesy of curtseying and gripped Georgiana by the hand. "I do declare, if we had not arrived so very quickly, I believe I should have broken my neck, the pathways are so icy." She turned and looked back at her brother. "I truly do believe they ought to do something about it."

Lord Hugh, divested of his outer garments, chuckled at his sister's comment, adjusting the cuffs of his shirt as he made his way towards them. "My dear Fran, how on earth do you expect the government to do anything about that? They cannot control the weather." He came to a halt and bowed. "Good afternoon to you, Miss Darcy. I trust you are well?"

"Very well indeed, thank you. I am surprised that you dared to venture out if the pavements are so perilous."

"Indeed, they are, Miss Darcy, but you see, my sister had me to help her," he replied with a warm smile brightening his face.

"And to own the truth," Lady Francesca added, "my brother could barely keep still at home. He was so restless; he just had to come here to visit with you."

Avoiding looking at either of the siblings, Georgiana felt the colour rising her cheeks. "Come on through to the drawing room. It's much warmer in there. We shall have tea."

As she rang the bell to call for tea, Georgiana admitted to herself that it was better to have company and some occupation than to continue her constant pacing of the house while waiting for Richard's return. Despite the fact that she was not overly fond of Lady Francesca, she would at least bring some gossip and help to while away the hours.

When the tea things arrived, along with a fruit loaf and more mince pies, Georgiana was glad there were more people to eat the cakes than just herself and Aunt Henrietta. The last thing she needed was to return to Derbyshire in the spring a few pounds heavier than when she left.

In fact, the DeVere siblings did bring gossip. Lady Francesca, with her voracious appetite for such news, barely gave Georgiana an opportunity to speak herself. As Lady Francesca regaled them with the shocking goings on in society, Georgiana's eyes strayed to Lord Hugh.

He was dressed in fawn trousers with a blue jacket and a beautiful deep wine-coloured brocade waistcoat. Her eyes traced the pattern, lingering a moment longer than they ought to have. As the firelight reflected off his cravat, she could tell it was made from the finest silk, tied expertly, by his valet no doubt, and secured in place with what she could only surmise was a diamond-studded pin. His sideburns were neatly trimmed and his hair fashionably tousled. For an instant, Georgiana imagined what it would be like to run her fingers through his reddish-brown hair. She was startled by her train of thought and the warmth that it produced spreading through her body.

Georgiana helped herself to another mince pie in her best effort to draw her mind away from Lord Hugh. It was to no avail, however, because as soon she picked up another pie, he followed suit, changing where he was seated and repositioning himself next to her on the settee.

Georgiana's heart thumped. She could barely breathe from his proximity, let alone chew the mouthful of sweet pie.

"My sister can certainly prattle on, can't she?" Lord Hugh whispered, leaning closer to Georgiana so that she stopped breathing altogether.

She could not respond and was scarcely able to raise her eyes to his.

"I do apologise."

"It is fine. My aunt likes to hear about the *ton*," Georgiana responded hoarsely.

Still leaning into her, he replied, "That was not what I was apologising for."

Georgiana's heart was beating so loudly she would have sworn the whole room could hear it.

"I seem to have quite an overpowering effect on you, Miss Darcy."

He held her gaze, and Georgiana could not have looked away if she tried. This time, the heat in her cheeks spread downwards.

"Do not be alarmed, my dear Miss Darcy. I feel the same way about you."

The room tilted, and Aunt Henrietta and Lady Francesca disappeared. As far as she was concerned, she and Lord Hugh were the only ones in the room.

"I want to tell you how ardently and deeply I have come to feel for you since our first meeting, Miss Darcy."

Georgiana swallowed.

"You must know how I feel." His eyes scanned her face as he spoke, searching for a hint of recognition.

"I..." Her mouth had gone so dry that she could not speak, let alone formulate what she wished to say.

"If, by some impossible misfortune, you do not know how I feel, please allow me to tell you and show you every day for the rest of our lives."

Georgiana could feel her mouth falling open and snapped it shut before she drew attention to herself.

Lord Hugh his face closer to hers. "You understand what I'm saying, do you not, Miss Darcy?"

To own the truth, Georgiana did not know for certain what he was trying to say. *Is he declaring himself? Is he proposing marriage to me?* Again, she swallowed and frowned, unable to speak.

"I see my declaration has taken you quite by surprise." He reached out with his free hand and laid it upon hers. "Please forgive me for the force of my passions. I am not accustomed to hiding what I feel. I believe it is better to make one's intentions known rather than to dissimulate and leave the lady unsure and in danger of having a broken heart."

Georgiana observed him closely as he spoke. She could not detect any dissimulation in his speech or his manner. She softened towards him. The temporary paralysis that gripped her fled, and she found herself smiling up at him. "I believe I understand what you mean, Lord Hugh."

"I am glad to hear it. I would not wish to leave here today without you knowing the ardour of my growing affection for you." He gave her hand a squeeze before withdrawing it. "I think we understand each other now, do we not?"

His voice was husky, and Georgiana noticed a line of perspiration above his top lip. Slowly she nodded. "Yes," she replied, unsure if she did indeed understand him.

"Georgiana, dear," Lady Francesca's voice cut through, snapping the pair back to the drawing room. "Your aunt was just telling me that she is planning a dinner party and that Hugh and I will be invited."

Georgiana blinked rapidly. "Oh, yes, she is."

"How absolutely delightful it will be!" Lady Francesca clapped her hands together. "These long cold nights can be such a bore if we are all housebound. Let us hope the doomsayers in the broadsheet newspapers are all wrong and we are not in for the worst winter ever. It would be such a crying shame if snow prevented us from attending the dinner party." She reached out and patted the cushion beside Aunt Henrietta. "It would not do at all, my dear Lady Matlock, for you to be stuck inside with no company and entertainment all winter long." She straightened up and shook her head, making her perfect curls bounce. "That is not what we come to London for, is it? We come here to make merry. If all we are to do is to sit in front of a blazing fire every single night, we could have stayed at home with Mama and Papa." She looked heavenward and rolled her eyes. "How absolutely tedious that would be! Endless rounds of whist and listening to Father read." She giggled. "What a happy little party we shall be!"

"Indeed, we shall," Lord Hugh agreed with his sister, his eyes still firmly locked on Georgiana's face. "We should all have a delightful time this winter," he drawled.

* * *

Richard and Alex could see the small hamlet Maisie had alluded to up ahead and slowed their pace, bringing their horses to a gentle trot. The steeds seemed to appreciate the slower pace, their breath fogging the air as they moved.

Richard continued to feel guilty. He had never driven a horse so hard in his life. He regretted it but only hoped his own horse was being well looked after and was recovering. Still, right now his attention was on the row of houses to the right side of the road. In the centre sat one that was larger than the others. He surmised that was where the family were now abiding. He mulled over what he would say, knowing there would be no easy way to go about it.

They tethered the horses at the gate and strode up to the front door. No doubt the whole village knew of their arrival by now. Alex, taking a quick look at Richard, rang the doorbell.

It felt like they waited an eternity before the door was answered. They could hear movement behind it and frantic whispering. Then, very slowly, the door was opened a crack by a young girl.

"Who is it?" she asked.

Richard cleared his throat. "My name is Colonel Fitzwilliam, and this is Mr Salisbury. We wish to speak to your father, Mr Ainsworth."

The young girl's little eyes widened at the sound of their family name. Hurriedly, she shut the door again and could be heard crying out, "Papa, there are some gentlemen to see you!"

Alex grinned and muttered, "They cannot avoid answering the door now." He lowered his voice even more, "We know they are in there."

"And we know we have the correct house."

Alex nudged him in the ribs. "Turn around very slowly and take a look at the cottage behind us on the other side of the street."

Richard did as he was bid as nonchalantly as possible, and there he could see opposite them two old ladies peering out from behind the curtains of their cottage. He doffed the rim of his top hat at them. Immediately they shot back out of view.

Richard turned back to face the Ainsworth's front door, chuckling to himself.

"Villages, eh?"

Just then the door opened and before them stood a tired and worn-looking man that Richard guessed to be in his late fifties.

"Good day to you, gentlemen. How may help you?" he asked, his voice just as tired as his face.

"Mr Ainsworth?" Richard asked.

"Yes?"

Richard and Alex looked at each other before Richard pressed on. "We are come to enquire about your daughter Margaret."

Mr Ainsworth went ghostly white. "I... I... I'm sorry, but... I..."

"We mean you and your family no harm, I can assure you," Richard blurted. "We merely wish to ask a few questions and to see if we can be of any assistance."

Mr Ainsworth's face turned from ghostly white to angry red in an instant. "We do not need charity. I'm sorry, but you've wasted your time."

He made to close the door, but Richard was quicker and stepped over the threshold. "Forgive me, Mr Ainsworth, but this is important."

Richard did not like forcing entry into the man's home, but he felt he had no alternative. They needed to know whether Lord Hugh was the father of the child or not.

As though sensing Richard's train of thought, a baby could be heard crying somewhere upstairs. He turned and watched as Mr Ainsworth latched the door behind them. "Again, I apologise. We wish to speak to you and Miss Ainsworth."

"Mrs Murray," the old man corrected him.

Richard inclined his head. "Right you are. We would like to speak to yourself and Mrs Murray."

As Alex fiddled with the rim of his top hat in his hands, Richard studied Mr Ainsworth's face. He had never seen a person looking so careworn. His heart went out to him. He knew the best thing he could do was to go along with the ruse that Margaret was indeed a widow and the babe's father was dead.

Mr Ainsworth disappeared back out into the hallway. Placing their hats and coats over the back of a chair beside the fireplace, Richard and Alex seated themselves. They did not wait long before the old man returned with his young daughter.

Richard was surprised when he saw her. *Dear God, she looks so much like Georgiana!*

The two of them rose and bowed in greeting.

"Mrs Murray, it is a pleasure to make your acquaintance," Richard said.

The young lady curtsied and hurriedly sat down as far away from the pair as was physically possible in the small drawing room.

"Well, what do you want?" Mr Ainsworth asked, hovering protectively beside his daughter's chair.

Richard looked down at his hands. Now they were there, he scarcely knew where to begin. "I beg your indulgence, Mrs Murray, but there is no easy way to do this, so I must come straight to the point. You recently resided in Richmond, did you not?"

She looked up at her father and then nodded.

"Where you were safely delivered of a boy. Is that so?"

Again, the young lad's cries from above stairs answered the question for her.

In the tiniest voice, she replied, "Walter. His name is Walter."

"She named the lad after me," Mr Ainsworth added, puffing out his chest.

"It is a good name," Alex replied.

Taking a deep breath, Richard plunged in. "Is the infant's father Lord Hugh DeVere?"

Margaret whimpered in panic, looked back at her father, and burst into tears. "We are found out! I am ruined!"

Mr Ainsworth's eyes bulged in his head and he stepped forward threateningly. "How dare you come into my house and make accusations of that sort!"

Richard held up his hands defensively. "I mean no harm by it, I assure you. We have travelled all the way from North London simply to ascertain the truth before Lord Hugh..." Richard could not finish a sentence. His throat clamped tightly shut and his eyes stung with tears.

Alex shuffled to the edge of the chair. "It's his cousin, you see? We want to prevent it happening again to her."

Richard stared at Margaret who continued to weep, her hands covering her face.

"I can tell by the looks of the two of you that the Colonel's cousin is a woman of means and a gentle lady, I am sure." Mr Ainsworth breathed heavily through his nose. "I doubt very much he would try something so underhanded as getting her with child as he did with my Maggie."

"No..." Richard's voice cracked with emotion. "But he might very well be after her dowry. And if our estimation of his reputation is correct, I doubt he will be a very faithful husband."

Mr Ainsworth studied Richard's face. The latter resisted the urge to look away. He wanted the old man to see the pain on his face and anguish he felt over protecting his cousin.

"You're right there." Mr Ainsworth's face screwed up in disgust. "He is a scoundrel and I doubt he would ever change his ways. She's not the only girl he's put in the family way, I can tell you." He put his arm about his daughter's shoulders. "He's done my girl wrong. He's damaged what can never be fixed. That's why we moved here." His eyes traversed the room. "Here we can start again. Here she is Mrs Murray, the widow, and little Walter is an orphan. My youngest, Charlotte—you saw opening the door—won't be marred by this scandal if we can keep up the deception."

"I can assure you, Mr Ainsworth, that we have no intention of doing or saying anything that would cause your family any more hurt."

"I won't be responsible for my actions, Colonel, if you even tried it," his eyes welled with tears. "I'll not have my daughter ruined forever, I tell you!" he shouted through gritted teeth.

Richard stood. "I would never put your daughter or her reputation in harm's way. I would like to offer my assistance, if I may."

Mr Ainsworth visibly deflated and sat down heavily in the chair beside his daughter, knocking Richard's gloves to the floor. "We thought he was going to ask for her hand in marriage," he said, his head bowed to his knees. "He courted her all proper like."

Richard and Alex stole a quick glance at each other, both of them unwilling to speak in case they stopped the old man from telling the story.

It turned out that their suspicions were correct. Lord Hugh had made overtures to the young Margaret, with the intention of bedding, not wedding, her.

Richard felt sick to his stomach that a woman could be used so poorly.

When the Duke of Somerset discovered his son's dalliance, he demanded that he marry a rich lady within the year. He was warned never to see Margaret again.

Richard watched on helplessly as the young woman sobbed into her hands—her heart clearly shattered.

After being warned off in a letter from the Duke, which Mr Ainsworth said they could read, they devised the strategy of claiming she was a widow and the boy was orphaned.

Richard knew that, unless Lord Hugh married the girl, there was no other viable course of action for the family to take.

The old man rose, unlocked the bureau standing in the corner of the room, and produced the letter. He handed it to Richard, who immediately recognised the seal of the Duke of Somerset.

It was all true. Alex had not told him gossip at all, but hard facts, back at his London townhouse. Richard felt nauseated.

"Forgive me for being impertinent, Mr Ainsworth, but what of your income?" Alex asked.

"I left my position at the bank. I only have a small income. A mere one hundred pounds per annum," he rubbed nervously at his neck.

"Then how can you afford this house?" Alex prodded further.

"It belonged to my wife's father, the village doctor here. He passed away last year." He looked at his daughter. "I had thought to sell it, but we need it now."

"That is fortunate indeed," Alex breathed.

"Aye, 'tis."

Richard asked if they could see the infant. When Margaret fetched him and brought him into the drawing room, there was no doubt in anyone's mind whose child he was. The shock of reddish-brown hair was enough of a telltale sign of his patronage.

They shared a meal together and, when they were finally ready to depart back to London, both Alex and Richard felt they ought to do more. Their departing words were that they would be in touch by letter. Richard was determined to do right by the wronged girl. He just did not know what or how.

Fourteen

Georgiana's head was in a spin. She tried to deny it, but she wondered if she was falling in love. As their guests departed, she stood by the window looking out into the street. Dark, heavy clouds were gathering to the east, and Georgiana conjectured as to whether they would have snow that night. While she stood watching, the first spots of rain splashed against the windowpane. Then another and another, until she noticed they were icy.

"Pining the loss of your beau already?" Aunt Henrietta chuckled as she came up beside her.

"No, I was watching the sleet. It will be another cold night, for sure."

"Come now," the older lady said, slipping her arm through Georgiana's. "You cannot fool me. You're watching Lord Hugh's carriage make its way down the street."

Georgiana bristled at the insinuation she had lied. She turned her head and glared at her matronly aunt as she continued to stare at the windowpane herself.

"There is nothing to be ashamed of." Aunt Henrietta kept her eyes ahead. "He is quite a catch, you know. You will make a fine couple and have all of society envious of you both."

Georgiana did not know what to say. *Was she listening in to what Lord Hugh said to me?*

"How exciting it will be to have another wedding in the family!" Aunt Henrietta finally turned and gazed upon her niece. "You will make such a beautiful bride," she said reaching up and stroking Georgiana's cheek.

Unable to help herself, Georgiana blushed.

"What did he say to you when he joined you on the settee," she asked, removing her hand from Georgiana's face. "Did he declare his intentions?"

Georgiana shook her head. "I cannot quite rightly say. It is all a blur to me. I believe..." She touched her own cheeks, the coolness of her fingers refreshing her red-hot face. "I believe he declared affection for me, but other than that..." She continued to shake her head.

"It is always confusing for a lady, is it not?" Aunt Henrietta smiled kindly, her eyes full of wisdom. "Men believe they have told us everything we need to know, but what a lady really needs to hear are the words plainly and simply—I love you and will you marry me?"

Georgiana burst out laughing. "Yes, the whole thing would be a great deal easier if men would just speak plainly instead of in poetic, flowery language."

Aunt Henrietta led her back towards the fireplace. "And what about your affections, my dear? Are you in love with Lord Hugh?"

Georgiana was uncomfortable as she sat down on the armchair on the opposite side of the fireplace. She was not accustomed to such direct questions, even from a family member. "I believe I like him very much, and he is prodigiously handsome."

"Like him?" Aunt Henrietta laughed. "You like him very much. Liking someone very much is not the same as being in love with them, Georgiana."

"I know, Aunt." Georgiana fiddled with her skirt over her knees and recalled her conversation with Lord Hugh. "I certainly feel as though I am in love when I am around him, and then..."

"And the pair of you have all the appearance of being in love."

"As to whether my heart is truly attached to Lord Hugh upon so short an acquaintance, I cannot say."

She looked up at her aunt desperately. "I would not wish to marry a man whom I did not love ardently. What I want, what I should so dearly wish for, is a love like Fitzwilliam and Elizabeth have."

Aunt Henrietta nodded slowly. "I believe their path to matrimony was not an easy one."

"You are right, even though Elizabeth always tells it with a smile on her face." Georgiana looked back towards the window, gazed through it, and instantly in her mind she was back at Pemberley with her brother and new sister-in-law. "Their love is so deep that I believe they would do anything for each other. In fact, if I'm not mistaken, Fitzwilliam did everything in his power to gain Elizabeth."

"Well, I do not know anything about that," Aunt Henrietta replied. "But I do know this. If he did everything in his power to gain the woman he loves, then he truly loves. Does not the Bard say *Love is not love Which alters when it alteration finds, Or bends with the remover to remove*?"

"Hmm..." Georgiana looked back at her aunt, a smile lighting up her face. "Shakespeare. I've always loved Sonnet 116."

"He goes on to tell us that love is steadfast and unchanging. If this is what you have or wish to have with Lord Hugh, or with any gentleman that you decide to marry, my dear, then you must give it time." She leant forward. "Heed my advice, child. I wish only the best for you, and I would not wish you married to anyone undeserving of your love or whom you did not love as ardently as Fitzwilliam and Elizabeth do each other." She smiled. Her eyes were warm and kindly. "You are young still. There is plenty of time. But most of all, I wish you to be very happy in marriage. Very few women have that opportunity. However, it is up to you. It is in your hands."

Slowly, Georgiana nodded, feeling the weight of her aunt's words. "You are right, Aunt. There is no hurry to marry." She returned her aunt's smile. "I do not know what has come over me. I lose my head when he is around."

"Enjoy this season, Georgiana. Enjoy falling in love with Lord Hugh, if that is what is happening to you. But remember that you wish for ardent love, deep love, everlasting love. Do not compromise." The older woman stood. "Now, if you will excuse me, I wish to take a nap. I will join you for dinner tonight."

"Very well, Aunt. Sleep well."

Left alone in the drawing room, Georgiana stared into the flames dancing in the fireplace and pondered her aunt's advice. She was right. Georgiana Darcy would not settle for anything less than the deepest and most fervent love. Of that she was certain. Therefore, as she too felt her eyelids heavy and sleep drawing in, she determined to slow things down a little with Lord Hugh. *After all, we barely know each other.*

She leant back and settled into the plush armchair, a smile playing on her lips as she started to doze off to sleep. Her mind drifted to her cousin Richard yet again. She wondered what was so urgent to take him away from London so rapidly. As she heard another icy blast batter the windowpane, she wondered if the weather would prevent Richard and Alex from reaching home as quickly as they had predicted.

The room was dark, the curtains were shut, and all the candles were lit by the time Georgiana awoke a few hours later. She shifted in the chair, stretching her stiff limbs, and realised someone at some point had covered her with a blanket and rebuilt the fire.

She smiled sleepily, glad she had come to London for the Christmas season. As she sat up, there was but one thing on her mind, *How soon will Richard return?*

Fifteen

The journey home was more laborious than they had anticipated. The wind increased, and the rain fell incessantly, turning to sleet before they reached London. Richard's face hurt. It stung from the icy droplets assaulting them as they rode on to their destination. Stopping each time to change the horses, they were beyond glad to enter an inn to warm themselves through by the fire. By the time they stopped to recover their own steeds, their stomachs rumbled and their hands and feet were like blocks of ice.

"You'd best not tarry if you want to get to London town before this storm really sets in," the barkeep advised, handing them two flagons of ale and two bowls of soup.

Alex looked up at the window. "He's right, you know. That sleet is now turning to snow."

Richard's brow furrowed. The last thing he wanted was to have to spend the night outside London. He wanted to get back to Pembroke Square. He hoped earnestly to prevent an attachment before Georgiana gave away her heart to a man Richard believed to be a worthless fortune hunter.

"Well, eat up. There's more in the kitchens if you want. And," the barkeep wiped his chubby hands on the grubby apron skirt, "we have one last room available, but you have to be quick. I imagine most folks travelling into London are going to stop tonight."

Richard nodded once. "We shall eat and depart immediately. I thank you for your kind attentions, but the truth is we must get home tonight."

"Fair enough. Suit yourselves. You know where to find me if you need me."

Once the barkeep had returned behind the bar and was happily chatting away with his other patrons, Alex leant forward. "Why the hurry?"

"I...just..." Richard sighed. He returned the spoon to the bowl of soup. He locked eyes with his friend and hoped Alex could read how sincere he was. "I need to get back. I need to let Georgiana know what kind of man Lord Hugh is."

Alex swallowed his mouthful of food. "And how exactly do you plan to do that? You can't just go in there and blurt it out.

You need to be tactful, Richard. If your cousin, Miss Darcy, is in love with Lord Hugh, who are you to prevent it?"

Richard thought of every excuse under the sun to counter Alex's question; however, he knew he was right. If Richard burst in after Georgiana had already given her heart to Lord Hugh, he would only cause derision and strife. Most likely, she would not forgive him for trying to interfere in her happiness. He had to slow down and think carefully.

"Do you want to stay overnight?" Alex asked.

"No." Richard rubbed at his face, the feeling coming back into his numb nose. "I still want to get back tonight. But," he paused, "you are right. I cannot just blurt it out. We have to think of what to do."

Alex washed his mouth out with ale. "It might be a good idea to find out what the man's intentions are towards your cousin first."

Richard stared at him hard.

"It may very well be that he is in love with her. For real this time. Let us not make him desperate."

"Very rarely have I ever met a man who changes his behaviour so very quickly, and especially not after a severe warning from his own father." Richard remembered all he knew about George Wickham.

"I agree with you on that. Generally that is the case. In this case, your cousin's heart is at stake. Let's not be responsible for breaking it. Let us bide our time, a week or two at most. We will watch him and find out what it is he wants. If he is only after your cousin's fortune and is keeping a doxy, then we will know what to do."

Richard sat back in the chair and puffed out his cheeks.

"And if he does not keep a doxy and is not after your cousin's fortune, then we must leave very well alone." Alex held Richard's gaze. "I also believe it would be best to keep *Mrs Murray's* existence from your cousin for the time being."

Richard nodded. "Agreed."

* * *

Georgiana heard the rapping at the front door and the ringing of the bell. Her knife and fork clattered onto the plate, and she was on her feet in a flash. Before dinner was called, the sleet had turned to heavy snow. When Aunt Henrietta descended the stairs after her nap, she was agitated and worried for her son.

Georgiana had assured her that, should they have been caught in the worsening weather, that Richard and Alex would have found shelter for the night. This did little to allay her fears. At the sound of the banging on the door, Georgiana straightaway believed the gentlemen had returned.

As she rushed headlong into the entrance hall, she encountered Hobbs walking sedately and rhythmically towards the front door. She halted and clasped her hands in front of her. It would not do to panic. *If they are home, they are home, safe and well.*

In a matter of seconds, the door was opened to reveal Richard and Alex, covered from head to foot in snow.

Upon seeing them safely returned, a sense of relief rushed through Georgiana, and she burst out laughing. "My goodness! You both look like snowmen!"

Glancing up at her as he stamped the snow off his boots on to the doormat, Richard's face lit up and he chuckled. "I expect we do."

"I know one thing for sure," Alex added. "I'm chilled to the bone."

"Oh, my dear boy," Aunt Henrietta said as she walked past Georgiana. Immediately the experience of her long years as a mother and the mistress of her own home took over. She turned to Hobbs. "Have hot water prepared, baths drawn up, and light the fires in both my son's room and the guestroom adjoining it." She then addressed Alex. "You shall stay here tonight. I cannot brook the thought of your going out in that weather again. This blasted winter!"

Alex did not resist. He continued to remove his outerwear and his boots.

"I do not know, for the life of me, what could have been so important to take you away from home, knowing what the newspapers were warning about this winter." Aunt Henrietta tugged at the lace handkerchief in her hands.

"Mama, you know I cannot divulge that information, but trust me, the trip was necessary." He leant in and kissed her on the cheek.

"Oh! Your face is like ice!" She pulled away from him. "Quick, the pair of you, get upstairs and get changed into some dry clothing. Hobbs will bring you some food and you can take a hot bath." She stole a quick glance towards the drawing room.

Georgiana observed that Aunt Henrietta's face was pinched and her worry lines were deeper.

"If you are both feeling up to it, you may join us in the drawing room afterwards. I'm sure a little port will warm your bellies nicely."

"Yes, Mama," Richard replied, his eyes firmly on Georgiana as he headed towards the staircase. Just the sight of her warmed his heart.

"Yes, Lady Matlock," Alex bowed as he shuffled in wet socks across the polished wooden floor.

The two ladies stood staring mutely up the staircase and watching the ascent of the gentlemen until they disappeared into the darkness beyond.

"Well, at least they are at home now," Georgiana spoke, her voice quiet.

"Let us pray that neither one catches their death of cold." Aunt Henrietta walked past her niece and back into the dining room.

Georgiana wondered for a moment if anyone did, indeed, die of cold anymore. A little fluttering started in her heart. She clasped her hands tighter together and said a little prayer for Richard and Alex's health.

Sixteen

The following day was a flurry of activity as they prepared for the dinner party. Aunt Henrietta invited Richard's friend Louis Ashton and his sister, Mrs Nicolette Fotheringhay. Also on the guest list were the DeVeres, Alex Salisbury, and Alex's promised bride-to-be, Miss Rebecca Hardwick, the daughter of a wealthy mill owner from the north of England. Georgiana believed she had made Miss Hardwick's acquaintance the summer before at a garden party her Aunt and Uncle Matlock held at their home.

Aunt Henrietta thought long and hard about the guest list and, in Georgiana's opinion, it had been designed with her in mind. Apart from Aunt Henrietta, there were four young ladies: Georgiana, Lady Francesca, Mrs Fotheringhay, and Miss Hardwick. Their male counterparts were Richard, Alex, Louis, and Lord Hugh. For such a small dinner party, Georgiana assumed the intention was for a little dancing.

She was not wrong in her assumption when she observed the drawing room being rearranged and Aunt Henrietta's beloved spinet being carried in. Georgiana knew her aunt was in her uncle's study, hiding from all the hustle and bustle. She did not like upheaval.

The day continued in much the same vein. The doorbell rang constantly with deliveries of flowers, coal for the fire, and food for the kitchens. The family ate their meals in the breakfast room; and, when it was time for Georgiana to prepare for the party, she found herself reluctant and not at all excited.

"Is there anything amiss, Miss Darcy?" Meg asked her as she helped her change undergarments.

"Would you believe me if I told you that I was not particularly enthused about tonight's party?" Georgiana asked, watching her maid's reflection in the long looking glass she stood before.

"But Colonel Fitzwilliam's friends and your new acquaintances will be there," Meg replied, her brows knit together.

Georgiana leant against the dressing table as Meg tied the fastenings behind her. "You are right." *So why would I be perfectly happy if tonight's soirée was cancelled entirely?* she asked herself.

Stepping into the scarlet dress with lace trimmings, she gazed at her own reflection. She greatly admired this dress, carefully chosen by herself and Elizabeth. Suddenly, the merriment of the season came upon her. She smiled. "This dress makes me feel decidedly Christmassy." She giggled. "Is Christmassy a word?"

"I can't rightly say, Miss," Meg giggled in return as she fastened the buttons on the back of Georgiana's dress. "I'm no expert on such things, but I do catch the meaning. It's a nice feeling. I do love this time of the year."

Georgiana's mind took her back to Pemberley and all the Christmases she could remember. "Yes, this time of the year has a special sort of magic to it, doesn't it?"

"Yes, Miss, it does."

Georgiana slipped on her long silk gloves as Meg attended to her hair. She decided on a simple style, making the most of her natural curls. However, she conceded that such a beautiful dress deserved hair adornments to crown it. She opened the drawer in the dressing table and withdrew a flat box covered with duck-egg blue damask. The corners were now a little tatty and threadbare and the clasp stuck. The jewellery box had once belonged to Georgiana's mother, Lady Anne Darcy. Now it was one of Georgiana's most prized possessions.

Carefully she opened the lid, revealing a selection of jewellery and hair ornaments, some having belonged to her mother, some newer pieces. She knew which she wanted. Inside she found six hairpins with diamond stars on their ends. She wore them every Christmas.

Georgiana twisted on the stool and handed them to Meg.

Her mother had also owned a simple matching necklace and bracelet, each with a single star made of diamonds. She traced a finger over the cool surface of one of the little stars, remembering the last time she saw her mother wear them. That had been the last Christmas they had celebrated together. Once she was old enough to be trusted with the precious jewels, Georgiana had religiously worn them each year since. Somehow, they made her feel as though her mother was there beside her. The thought filled her with courage.

Below stairs, Georgiana could hear the sounds of the guests arriving. She was surprised at their earliness.

Her coiffure finished, she stole a quick glance towards the window. The curtains were shut, and she could not see the weather beyond. "Is it snowing?" She asked Meg.

The lady's maid shuffled to the window and peeked through the curtains. Georgiana caught a glimpse of one of the streetlamps outside, casting a faint yellow glow from the candlelight.

"Not that I can see, Miss Darcy."

Meg returned to the dressing table and helped Georgiana with the necklace and bracelet. Then Georgiana stood and admired her reflection in the mirror.

"Now it feels like Christmas has begun." She beamed, her cheeks rosy from a little dab of rouge pomade. Her lips and eyes were also treated to a touch of makeup, prepared from natural ingredients by Meg. She moved her head from side to side, contenting herself that the little application of cosmetics was not overly done. Then she turned and slid her feet into little satin pumps that were comfortable enough for dancing. "There!" she declared triumphantly. "I believe I am ready."

"Indeed, you are, Miss. I hope you have a grand evening."

"Thank you, Meg," Georgiana replied, heading towards the door.

Downstairs in the entrance hall, Georgiana found her cousin Richard and Alex in deep discussion as she descended the stairs. As soon as the pair caught sight of her, they stopped talking and stood in admiration.

Alex whistled. "My word!"

"Indeed," Richard whispered, stepping forward and offering Georgiana his hand.

Georgiana blushed to the roots of her hair.

"You are looking decidedly beautiful this evening," Richard cooed.

Georgiana could feel her blush deepening and her cheeks red hot. *I needn't have applied any rouge.* "Thank you, Richard." She took his hand, and he led her into the drawing room where she found everyone else was already assembled.

"Miss Darcy!" Lady Francesca's voice rang out. "How absolutely delightful you look!" The lady in question made her way around the furniture and towards Georgiana. Once standing before her she leant forward and kissed her on the cheek.

Georgiana wondered when they had become so familiar as to greet one another with a kiss. "And you look as wonderful as you always do," she responded in kind.

Without seeing him move, Lord Hugh appeared at his sister's elbow. "I wholeheartedly agree with my sister. You look delightful this evening, Miss Darcy." Lord Hugh bowed and reached out to kiss the back of her gloved hand.

Georgiana smiled shyly, basking in their compliments. "Thank you. You are too kind."

As Lord Hugh straightened up, he held her gaze. "I assure you, I am most sincere."

At the intensity of his gaze, Georgiana felt uncomfortable. She took a half-step towards Richard, who remained by her side. His compliments did not fill her with a warmth and excitement as Richard's had. Suddenly she felt a little nauseated. Her smile lost some of its brilliance.

"Would you like a glass of sherry?" Richard asked her, tightening his grip on her hand.

His touch was reassuring. She nodded. "Please."

As her cousin led her away, Georgiana wondered what had just happened. She realised with alacrity that it was Lord Hugh's attentions which caused such unease. While she watched Richard pour the Spanish liqueur into the crystal glass, she pondered the sensation. Revelation hit her like a runaway horse. *I am not in love with Lord Hugh.* Her mouth fell open. *I am not in love with him at all.* She closed her mouth again and gratefully took the glass of sherry from Richard. She took a sip, not only enjoying the heat of the liquid as it slid down to her stomach, but also relishing the sense of relief that flooded her being. *I have enjoyed his flirtations and nothing more. My heart is wholly untouched by Lord Hugh.* She almost burst out laughing and her own thoughts.

"A penny for them." Richard's voice startled her.

"Sorry?" She blinked to clear her head.

"A penny for your thoughts," Richard replied, searching her face. "You are in deep thought, cousin."

"It is of no consequence, I assure you, but I have just realised something quite pleasing to myself."

Richards eyebrows rose. "And am I permitted to ask what this realisation is?"

Georgiana giggled. "You are permitted to ask, but whether or not I shall furnish you with an answer is another matter."

The couple laughed, drawing the attention of the DeVere siblings.

"What is so funny?" Lady Francesca approached, her brother in tow.

"Oh," Richard replied quickly, "it is nothing. Just a family joke, really. It would take a long time to explain it."

Georgiana watched Lady Francesca's expression turn from affable to what she could only describe as quite put out.

"We were merely reminiscing about something that happened one Christmas when I was a young girl."

Lady Francesca smiled, although it did not reach her eyes. "Oh, I see." She turned to her brother and laid a perfect hand upon her brother's arm. "My brother and I often indulge in such remembrances."

Georgiana felt iciness emanate from the lady.

Richard deftly changed the subject. "Lady Francesca, do you and Lord Hugh often travel back home to Somerset?"

A look of disgust crossed Lady Francesca's face. "Oh!" she fairly squawked. "Not at all! My brother and I despise the countryside." She pulled a face that made her look as though she had eaten a particularly bitter lemon. "All those bugs, hardly any diversion at all, and such limited acquaintance! No, Colonel Fitzwilliam, we do not travel to our estate in Somerset often. In fact," she grimaced, "we avoid it like the pox, preferring London or Bath."

Georgiana watched on mutely as not a single muscle moved in Richard's face.

"Oh, you do surprise me. I have heard tell that Somerset is one of England's most beautiful counties," he quipped.

"There is no doubt about it. It is beautiful." Lady Francesca turned her body and surveyed the rest of the room as though bored with the conversation. "But other than Bath, the rest of the county is tedious beyond measure, I can assure you. I prefer to live in town."

"And yet," Richard continued, "it is such a relief to return home to the countryside after spending much time in a city, I find."

Georgiana could barely keep her countenance. Richard slighted Lady Francesca with nary an attempt at disguising it. "Let us be seated," she interjected before Lady Francesca could respond.

Georgiana joined Alex and his fiancée, Miss Hawkins, who were in conversation with Aunt Henrietta, and sat down beside the young lady.

Miss Hawkins turned towards her. "I believe we are acquainted somewhat," she said.

"I thought so," Georgiana shifted a little, moving her knees to the side. "Was it not the summer before last at Lord and Lady Matlock's summer garden party?"

"Indeed, it was. You have a very good memory, Miss Darcy."

"Did you accompany Mr Salisbury then?"

Miss Hawkins' face mirrored the colour of Georgiana's dress. "I did."

"Excuse my impertinence in asking, but were you affianced to him then?"

"Yes, I was." She took a deep juddering breath and suddenly the words came tumbling out. "It has been a long engagement. Not that Alex or I wanted such an arrangement. It's my father, you see."

Georgiana tilted her head. "Your father?"

"Yes," she nodded. "Alex comes from a long line of some of the most eminent lawyers in the land. My father wishes dearly to be certain to give me away in marriage in a manner that is equal to Alex's standing in society."

Georgiana was taken aback by the confession. "Surely that is of little consequence," she frowned. "If the families have agreed to the engagement, certainly they would be happy for the marriage to take place."

"But my father was not." She smiled weakly. "However, he has given his permission for us to finally wed this summer." Her smile took on a new life and lit up her face. "He is taking a wonderful house for us not five miles from where I grew up."

"How delightful! To be settled so close to one's family must give you such comfort, Miss Hawkins"

Miss Hawkins nodded. "You cannot imagine how worried I was at the thought of having to come and live in London always. I grew up near Manchester, but my father built our home in the countryside. I am not accustomed to city living."

Georgiana understood her perfectly.

"And please, Miss Darcy, do call me Rebecca. I believe we shall be good friends."

Her smile was disarming, and Georgiana could not help but compare Rebecca with Lady Francesca. "I am sure we shall." She returned the smile warmly. "And please call me Georgiana."

She looked up at the sound of Lady Francesca's laughter peeling through the air. It was not difficult to locate her; she had attached herself to Richard as soon Georgiana moved. The lady made no attempt at dissimulation of her intentions. It was evident she was flirting with him by the way she draped herself over his left arm and touched the buttons on his waistcoat. Richard, on the other hand, did not even look in her direction. She could see the colour rising in his neck. She knew from experience that only happened when he was irritated or frustrated.

She wished she could do something to help him, but Rebecca was already in the middle of telling her all about her wedding plans. Reluctantly, Georgiana looked away from her cousin and gave her new friend her full attention. As she listened on, she compared Rebecca and Alex's wedding preparations with those of the two familial weddings she could remember—her cousin Thomas, now the Earl of Matlock, and her own brother, Fitzwilliam.

Despite the girl coming from new money, Georgiana found herself becoming excited as Rebecca described the extravagance which her father was lavishing upon her.

When dinner was called, the whole ensemble marched slowly towards the dining room. Once there, Georgiana discovered herself, according to Aunt Henrietta's seating plan, to be between Lord Hugh and Louis. Inside she groaned. Since realising that she was not at all in love with Lord Hugh, Georgiana realised she had to do her best to distance herself from him.

As of now, she had to grin and bear it as best she could, as her brother would say. Thinking about him, her mind wandered to Hertfordshire while Lord Hugh hurried to her side and held her chair out for her.

Pulling herself away from the cosy, familial scene in her head, Georgiana smiled kindly at Lord Hugh. "Thank you."

As dinner was served, Lord Hugh bellowed, "What a delightful spread your aunt puts on!"

Aunt Henrietta could not fail to have heard him. "Thank you, Lord Hugh. I am gratified that you think so," she replied from the end of the table.

She caught Georgiana's eye. At first, the latter thought her aunt had something in her eye, but when she continued to give a discrete nod and wink towards her and Lord Hugh, she caught her drift. She was encouraging her niece to engage Lord Hugh in conversation.

Georgiana took a deep breath, sighed, and then, believing it to be the safest option, addressed both Louis and Lord Hugh at the same time. "Do you believe the snow will continue to fall and we'll have the horrendous winter the broadsheets are foretelling?"

She was grateful when Louis was the first to respond. "I was just talking to my sister on the way here about that very same thing, Miss Darcy. It does seem we are getting frightfully more snow here in London this year than we usually do. Wouldn't you say, Lord Hugh?"

The baton was passed, and Georgiana wondered if Louis would ever get another word in for the remainder of the evening.

Lord Hugh's face lit up like a thousand candles. He took a deep breath. "Interestingly enough, I have been reading an awful lot in the newspaper about the weather." Lord Hugh put his fork down. "There was some discussion in the gentleman's club last evening about some sort of volcano on the other side of the world."

"A volcano?" Louis asked leaning forward past Georgiana to get a better view of Lord Hugh.

"Indeed!" Lord Hugh nodded picking up his wine glass.

Georgiana squinted. "Forgive me, Lord Hugh, but I am unable to fathom how a volcano on the other side of the world could possibly cause such snow here in England."

Lord Hugh smiled patronisingly at her, then reached across and tapped her on the hand. "Of course I would not expect you to understand, my dear. How can a woman understand the sciences?"

Georgiana bit her lip and tasted blood.

"I shall endeavour to explain it as simply as I possibly can," he chortled.

Thankfully, he removed his hand before Georgiana could snatch hers away.

"Evidently, the volcano spews rock, lava, and ash into the air which then travels via the weather system around the world. It's quite fascinating."

"And this has affected the weather here in England how?" Louis asked.

Lord Hugh waved his hand in the air vaguely as though dismissing the question. "You know, dust and the like in the air, blocking out the sun, one fellow said."

"So no one rightly knows?" Louis asked.

Georgiana watched on as a little spark of satisfaction grew in her stomach when Lord Hugh's face turned the colour of beetroot.

"Well, I'm not a scientist per se." He cleared his throat. "Neither are most of the fellows in the gentleman's club." He swallowed while his eyes searched the ceiling for what to say. "But a lot of them are very intelligent chaps indeed. Old Oxford boys, a...and the like."

Georgiana speared a mussel on her plate, popped it into her mouth, and chewed, giving herself something else to do other than giggle at what Lord Hugh said. *He doesn't understand it either.*

"Well, it is terribly bad luck," Louis replied. "I hear things are especially tough in Wales and Ireland right now."

Georgiana swallowed and addressed Louis. "What do you mean?" She had never been one for reading the broadsheets. She would occasionally read an article or story that caught her attention, but she found most of the writing to be waffling and opinionated rather than dealing with cold, hard facts, which she preferred in a newspaper.

Louis explained, "I have heard tell that many people are going begging in the streets for food."

Georgiana's mouth fell open. She jumped, feeling Lord Hugh's hand upon hers again.

"Do not worry your pretty little head, Miss Darcy. They are only poor people, after all. There is nothing one can do about their plight."

Georgiana's blood boiled. "There is much one can do about the plight of the poor, Lord Hugh. I would have thought you of all people would understand that. We privileged few are in a position to aid them, are we not?"

To Georgiana's amazement Lord Hugh sat back in his chair and roared with laughter. She turned her head, looking between Louis and Lord Hugh. While the latter continued to laugh at her, the former's eyes were filled with pity and apology.

"Oh, dear me!" Lord Hugh cried, dabbing at the corners of his eyes with a napkin. "The things these ladies do say! What notions! What would you have us do?" He twisted in his chair to face her, his elbow leaning on the tablecloth. "Would you have them feed from our own tables and our own harvests?"

Georgiana felt as though she had been doused in icy cold water. "Actually, Lord Hugh, that is precisely what I would suggest. While we live in plenty and they have nothing, surely it is logical that we share what we can."

Lord Hugh sucked air in through his teeth. He lowered his voice conspiratorially. "I believe what you are saying is treasonous and revolutionary, Miss Darcy."

Her eyebrows rose. "On the contrary, Lord Hugh. What I'm saying is full of compassion for those who are starving and, I believe, what I suggest would be the Christian thing to do." Georgiana turned back to the plate before her, determined she would not speak to him again for the remainder of the evening. As she did so, she caught the expression of astonishment on his face. Clearly, he did not expect such a retort.

For the rest of the meal, Georgiana satisfied herself by conversing with her aunt, Louis, and Alex, who sat opposite her. Alex and Aunt Henrietta were discussing Alex's forthcoming nuptials. Louis and Georgiana, who were unmarried, had very little to add to the discussion. So, instead, they talked about the delights of London town in the winter.

Georgiana ate her meal in rapt fascination while Louis explained in more detail how his mother escaped revolutionary France. "I suppose your mother being French explains why you and your sister are called Louis and Nicolette," Georgiana said.

"Indeed, it is. Mother, or *maman* as she prefers to be called, has injected a rather large flavour of France and the French way into our home."

"How delightful! And where is home?"

"They live in Hertfordshire."

"Hertfordshire! My brother is residing there at the moment with my sister-in-law, Elizabeth. They are staying at Netherfield Hall near to the little town of Meryton. Do you know it?" she asked.

Louis exclaimed excitedly, "Know it? I know it very well. It is not more than ten miles from our home, I am certain of it."

The meal continued in much the same contented vein until the ladies rose and retired to the drawing room, leaving the men to their cigars and port.

The air in the drawing room was fresher than the heat and smells of the dining room. Georgiana fought a yawn as she and the ladies seated themselves around the fire.

Seventeen

Richard, now being left alone with Louis, Alex, and Lord Hugh, stretched out his legs underneath the table and relaxed a little. He had, of course, been on his best behaviour in deference to his mother, but spending the past two hours listening to the crooning and cooing of Lady Francesca was more than a little tiring.

Richard indicated to Hobbs that the port and cigars should be handed to the other gentlemen first, while he sat contentedly finishing the last of his glass of red wine. He watched Lord Hugh drinking heavily.

Alex and Louis, he was well acquainted with; however, he and Alex were also well acquainted with Lord Hugh's reputation. He wondered how he would keep his cool and maintain friendliness with the man when Alex struck up the conversation.

"I was surprised that your sister's husband, Lord Fotheringhay, was not invited," he said, earnestly attempting to light a cigar.

"I believe Lady Matlock did invite my brother-in-law. However," Louis closed his eyes and shook his head, "he very rarely ventures into society unless an invitation comes from one of his peers."

"I'm very disappointed to hear it," Alex replied, dragging hard on the cigar now it was lit.

"Your sister is happily settled, one supposes. It is a very happy match, is it not? After all, he is a member of the House of Lords." Alex prodded further.

"As my dear sister tells it, it is the worst decision she's ever made," Louis laughed, waving Hobbs on to fill his glass more than the butler deemed appropriate. "I don't need to tell you he's old enough to be her father but is as rich as Croesus. She is just one of those silly romantic types, I suppose."

"I quite like it that Rebecca has romantic notions," Alex added. "In fact, I find those notions add a little extra to our relationship. I think it is lamentable that part of your sister's character is not satisfied."

"Tish! Who cares if that part of a woman's character is satisfied or not," Lord Hugh scoffed, adding his tuppence worth. "Women's heads are full of such ridiculous notions, are they not?"

"Like love, marriage, and fidelity?" Richard could not resist adding.

"Ha!" Lord Hugh almost choked on his port. "Of course, love and marriage. They are part of one's duty, are they not?"

No one answered, but the other three gentlemen watched on as Lord Hugh clipped the end of his cigar and lit it, waiting for him to continue.

"But fidelity…come on!" He puffed a perfect 'oh' of smoke up into the air and watched as it floated towards the candelabra hanging from the ceiling. "No man can be expected to keep faithful, surely. Those vows are just ridiculous promises made in church to keep our womenfolk quiet, aren't they?"

"I, for one, shall take my vow of fidelity seriously," Alex replied, dangerously quiet.

Richard observed closely as Lord Hugh looked at Alex as though he had grown a second head.

"How singular!"

Alex looked quite offended. "Do you mean to say that, if you were to take a bride, you would not remain faithful to her?"

"Of course not! What fool of a man would?" His eyes challenged Alex across the table.

"So you would keep a mistress?" Louis asked, his brows knit together in one heavy line.

"I would not give up my fancies, as I like to call them." Lord Hugh sniffed. "The whole point in getting married is to continue the family line and, in so doing, hopefully bring a little more cash into the family coffers at the same time."

Richard felt his anger rise. The chair creaked as he squeezed the arm hard. *That is not just drunken folly talking.*

"When I marry, and I do intend to marry," Lord Hugh continued, "I shall marry a woman of wealth and of good breeding. I shall marry one who is handsome enough to keep me entertained long enough to produce progeny, and then I shall skedaddle back to London to indulge in my fancies." He dragged on his cigar.

While puffing his, Richard lost all taste for smoking. He discarded the barely touched cigar into an ashtray. *He's talking about Georgiana. He intends to marry Georgiana and discard her once she has produced him an heir.* Richard felt sick to his stomach. He scowled, swirling the remainder of the port in his glass.

Alex pushed the subject further. "What about the misfortune and possible embarrassment to your family if any of your mistresses have children?"

"What of it?" Lord Hugh shrugged. "As Father says, my responsibility lies only with my family. If any of my mistresses are foolish enough to get themselves with child, what is that to me?"

"Are you saying that you bear no responsibility whatsoever if any of your mistresses are pregnant?" Richard growled, his timbre low.

"What do you mean, if?" Lord Hugh guffawed.

Louis pushed his chair backward, coming to his feet. "You mean you already have a by-blow?"

"So what if I have? Haven't we all?" Lord Hugh continued to laugh loudly. No one else joined in.

Richard stood up. "I believe it is time we joined the ladies."

"Yes, we must do our duty and not keep them waiting," Lord Hugh replied, stubbing out his cigar, draining the last of his port and taking another glassful before rising.

Richard hung back as Lord Hugh exited, staggering tipsily.

"Dear God!" Louis sighed. "Doesn't he have his sights on your cousin, Miss Darcy?"

"Indeed, he has," Alex replied, making no attempt to hide the anger in his voice.

"Not for long," Richard added, stomping out of the room.

* * *

Once the gentlemen had joined the ladies in the drawing room, tea was served, and Lady Francesca suggested a game of charades. It was not something Georgiana was particularly talented at, so she was happy to allow their guests the limelight.

Again, she found Lord Hugh sitting beside her, overly attentive as usual, although she was convinced he was intoxicated. He made sure she had enough tea to drink and continuously asked her if she wanted anything more to eat or if she would like to move closer to the fire. "I'm quite all right, thank you," she replied repeatedly, trying to focus on the game and not Lord Hugh.

Georgiana laughed hard throughout the game, and finally Louis and Lady Francesca were declared joint winners.

"I declare, I do not know the last time I had such fun!" Lady Francesca called out to the room at large as she plumped herself down on the settee.

Georgiana had to agree. "I did not realise we were in company of some of Britain's greatest actors!" she commented breathlessly.

"I believe the only thing to make this a perfect night," Lady Fotheringhay joined, "is that if someone would play that beautiful instrument in the corner and we could dance."

Lady Francesca sat bolt upright. "Oh, what a splendid idea!" She swivelled around, and her eyes came to rest upon Aunt Henrietta.

Georgiana watched excitedly as her aunt guessed what Lady Francesca was about to ask.

"Would you, Lady Matlock?" Lady Francesca begged, pouting a little.

"You wish for me to play the spinet so that you young folk may dance?" Aunt Henrietta asked, barely concealing a smile.

"I have heard tell of what an excellent musician you are, Lady Matlock," Lady Francesca pushed her suit.

Georgiana was amused to see a blush rise upon her aunt's ageing cheeks.

"Very well," Aunt Henrietta responded, her eyes twinkling with merriment.

Georgiana arose from the settee, allowing the gentlemen to move the furniture to the edges of the room as Aunt Henrietta approached the mature instrument. She remembered as a child, staying with her aunt and uncle, that her aunt would play for hours. Music always filled their home. Every time they gathered as a family, it was Aunt Henrietta who stepped forward, the first to begin to play.

She did not ask which pieces of music the younger members of the party wanted to dance to. Instead, she immediately began to play the introduction to the piece Georgiana recognised as *Le Fugitif*, and all eight of those standing formed the quadrille and waited to begin.

To her astonishment, she discovered that she and Richard were the first pair to begin. She felt a little self-conscious as she trotted forward to meet Richard in the centre of the circle. However, as the others tapped their feet, clapped their hands, or moved gently to the music, Georgiana began to relax and enjoy it. It was the first time she had been in such close proximity to Richard in hours.

As the dance moved around each couple in turn, Georgiana noticed Lord Hugh doing his utmost to catch her eye and move as close to her as he physically could.

Georgiana breathed a sigh of relief when the dance was over, only to hear Aunt Henrietta begin to play *Marmion.* Again, Richard was faster than Lord Hugh in asking her to dance.

She caught sight of Lord Hugh's face and was persuaded she saw more than a little anger written upon it.

"You know, cousin, you ought to let me dance with the other gentlemen in the room. It is not politic to keep me all to yourself."

Richard laughed as they took their places. It was not until they passed close enough to each other that he could reply. "If I send you with the other gentlemen in the room, then I would not only deprive myself of the best dancer here for a partner, but I'd then have to dance with Lady Francesca."

Georgiana could not help but laugh. They were in two sets of four for this particular country dance, but Lady Francesca was not in theirs. Glancing at the said lady as she skipped past, Georgiana was left in no doubt that the Duke's daughter was irritated with having to dance with Louis Ashton. Unfortunately, spying upon Lady Francesca meant she was looking at the other set of four dancers and not taking care of where she was stepping. She almost crashed into Alex.

"Pay attention," Richard laughed, taking hold of her by the shoulders and putting her back on course.

With her cheeks burning with embarrassment, Georgiana concentrated on the dance, hoping no one had noticed. Lamentably, she caught sight of the smirk on Lord Hugh's face and suspected he would believe she was keeping her eyes firmly on him instead of giving her own dance partner her full attention.

By the time that dance finished, Georgiana was ready for refreshments. That desire was dashed when the cry of "Another" went up and Aunt Henrietta began to play *The Adieu.*

This time she and Richard danced in still closer proximity, and they had more time to talk. She was somewhat disappointed, though, when all he did was exchange pleasantries with her. She frowned up at his face, trying to fathom what he was about, when she saw the flicker of something deep, longing, and passionate in his eyes which made her step falter.

She was not naïve; she knew what that look meant. She was, nevertheless, surprised to see it in Richard. The even greater surprise was the reaction produced within her. Her heart began to beat faster, her breathing became shallower, and not because of the dance. She felt a lightning bolt strike straight through her to her deepest, innermost parts.

As a dance progressed, each time they passed each other and moved in unison, they closed the gap between each other. Georgiana was held mesmerised by his eyes. The desire building within her left her powerless to resist. She knew full well what she was feeling and could see emblazoned in Richard's eyes the same mounting hunger.

The dancers passed by in a blur until suddenly everything came to a stop. The room continued to spin. Richard caught her before she stumbled to the floor. She could see her own feeling of alarm mirrored in his eyes. *He wants me as I want him,* she thought, more than a little terrified of the intensity of it all.

Richard stepped back, bowed, and allowed another to take her hand for the next dance. Georgiana barely heard the music, let alone recognised with whom she was dancing. Her eyes, her mind, and her heart were firmly fixed upon Richard.

"Hang it all, Miss Darcy!" Lord Hugh's voice cut through the haze, bringing Georgiana back to the moment. "Are you dancing with me at all? Your head seems to be in the clouds." He pouted.

"I do beg your pardon, Lord Hugh," Georgiana responded, trying her hardest to snap out of it and join in the dance.

"I should jolly well hope so! A man could be quite put off by being ignored like this." His pout deepened as he whined.

Georgiana resisted the impulse to tell him she had already apologised, not wishing to inflate his ego any further than it already was.

He shuffled up closer to her as they moved around the room. Her instinct was to recoil. What she felt when Lord Hugh moved his body against her was a far cry from what she felt when Richard did it. Again, the thought of Richard sent the bolt of lightning through her stomach to the core of her being.

"What do you say to us stepping out onto the veranda at the back of the house to get a little bit of fresh air?" Lord Hugh asked.

Despite being overheated from dancing so long, Georgiana shivered as his eyes traced to the mounds of her breasts and along the cleavage between them. "I do not believe it would be a sensible idea to be outside in this weather for very long," she replied, grasping at straws.

"Nonsense! People do it all the time."

She looked up at him mustering as much defiance as she could. "But I do not."

"Dash it, Miss Darcy! Anyone would think that you're not violently in love with me!" He said loudly enough for the other couple to overhear.

She noticed Alex glaring at her. She wanted to scream. She had been flattered by Lord Hugh's attentions and for a moment she had lost her head. Perhaps she had erred in her behaviour towards and with him, but now it seems the man was unable to take the slightest hint of her indifference.

As they continued to dance, Alex glowered at her. She had no idea what she had done to offend him so, but his obvious ire upset her. Spinning around, she saw Richard dancing with Lady Francesca. Was he dancing as closely and as passionately with her as he had with Georgiana? Her stomach lurched. She felt sick.

Thankfully, the music stopped, the dance finished, and Georgiana fled from the room. She needed air. She needed to be able to breathe. She needed to think.

Eighteen

Richard did not know how he made it through the evening after dancing with Georgiana. His passions were inflamed. To fill his mind with something other than the carnal thoughts it was consumed with now, he gave in and danced with Lady Francesca. The lady could not have been happier. Richard believed she left everyone in the room with no doubt as to where her affections lay.

With every twist and turn, with every pass of their bodies, Lady Francesca did everything in her power to touch him. He would have to be a simpleton indeed to miss the message she was sending.

He kept his eyes firmly on his dancing partner, but his attention and his mind were still with Georgiana. Out of the corner of his eye, he could see her looking decidedly uncomfortable dancing with Lord Hugh. They were deep in conversation, it seemed, and Richard wished he knew what they were talking about.

His mind flashed back to Margaret Ainsworth, now styling herself Mrs Murray, and her little boy, Walter, and anger welled up inside him. He was astonished at how quick an antidote to passion his fury was. Now he wished, more than ever, to know what Lord Hugh was whispering to Georgiana as they danced.

He could only surmise that whatever it was, the lady was not impressed. As his mother finished playing on the spinet and the dance came to a stop, Georgiana fled the room. Thankfully, she was unseen by most. The dancers were hot and in need of refreshment. Richard rang the bell and, as soon as Hobbs arrived, he called for tea to be served. He did not see Lord Hugh slip out of the room after his cousin.

* * *

Georgiana fled directly to the dining room. She stood before the tiny tree on the sideboard and wondered how they had managed to stuff so many little paper roses between its branches. *The poor thing looks veritably swamped.*

Less than a minute ago, and rather loudly, Lord Hugh had said he believed she was violently in love with him. Mentally she kicked herself for being such a fool. She stamped her foot and groaned with the agony of it. She was not in love with Lord Hugh. She knew that more than ever now. But somehow within the last couple of weeks, and such a short acquaintance, Lord Hugh had decided they were both violently in love with each other.

Georgiana tensed. She gripped the edge of the sideboard until her knuckles went white at the sound of footfalls behind her. She was filled with dread. Instinctively, she knew it was Lord Hugh.

"There you are, my little petal."

His words made her skin crawl and she shivered.

"Are you cold? Shall I fetch your shawl?"

Planting the most pleasant smile she could muster on her face, Georgiana slowly turned around. "Why, Lord Hugh, that would be very kind of you, but I am not cold. I am overheated from the dancing."

As he took a step towards her, she sidestepped nearer the dining table.

"I must say," his voice a little husky, "that you do dance exceedingly well, dearest Georgiana. You've quite got my passions up."

She wished with all her heart they had not agreed to call each other by their first names when in private. She had promised herself she would never be so foolish as she had been with George Wickham. But now here she was in this situation, feeling just as imprudent, having acted naïvely. "Thank you. I have been blessed with some of the best tutors."

Lord Hugh chuckled and shifted his weight to lean closer. "I do not believe your excellence at dancing is to be attributed to the superiority of your tutors. I believe that is all your own natural talent, my dear."

It was meant as a compliment, but each word he uttered made her throat drier. "Oh, you flatter me," she replied, moving further to the left and putting a dining chair between them.

Lord Hugh laughed. "Of course I flatter you, my sweet. I intend to flatter you every day for the rest of our lives."

Georgiana's stomach somersaulted backwards. She did not know if she would faint or vomit. Her mind taunted her. She wondered what her brother would say to her about the pickle she had got herself into.

"Are you quite well?" he asked, reaching for her.

"I...perhaps I have simply overexerted myself this evening," she lifted her shoulder, avoiding his touch.

"Shall I fetch someone for you?" he pressed.

Georgiana shook her head. "No, that will not be necessary. I think I should return to the drawing room and take some refreshment." She made to walk around the back of the table.

"Maybe you merely need a little bit of affection," he responded, the huskiness returned to his voice.

Georgiana shuffled a little further around the table. "I am quite all right, I assure you."

"Come, come! Do not be like that. We are lovers, after all!" He closed the gap between them with long strides.

Georgiana was horrified. "We are most certainly *not* lovers, Lord Hugh." Using his title made her feel a little better and confident of putting an invisible barrier between them.

It appeared that he would not be dissuaded. He reached her side with one longer step and put his arm about her shoulder. "Oh, don't be so cold, Georgiana. It is obvious to myself and others, I am certain, how deeply you have come to feel for me."

He pulled her into an embrace. Georgiana wanted to scream but her throat clamped shut and she could barely move out of fear.

Lord Hugh pressed his advantage. "You and I will make a wonderful married couple, don't you think?"

No, I do not think! her mind screamed, her mouth still unable to utter a syllable.

"It is a good match on both sides, you must admit." He inched his head forward.

Georgiana was paralysed with terror. All she could see was his mouth as he bent his head for a kiss. As she felt his alcohol-filled breath upon her face, something snapped and her body was free. She tried to wriggle out of his grasp, but he tightened his grip, clamping her body to his. She could feel his arousal and the icy fingers of fear crept back in to claim her.

She was powerless. Lord Hugh's mouth was upon hers, wet, warm, and searching. She clamped her lips together, determined not to respond positively to his kiss.

"Come on, Georgiana," he muttered, pressing himself hard against her thigh. "Don't be such a cold fish." He continued kissing down to her neck. "I know we're not married yet, but allow a fellow a little bit of pleasure, won't you?"

Georgiana's eyes wide, she wriggled a little to free herself, but he took that as acquiescence.

"That's the spirit, my girl!"

Suddenly, he seemed to be possessed of more hands than was natural. One of them grasped her breast. In a flash, Georgiana was filled with anger. She twisted so violently that they both fell into one of the dining chairs sending it crashing to the floor. "Unhand me, you brute!" she screamed at the top of her voice.

What happened next was a blur. She heard the door open. She heard footsteps. Then she saw Richard grabbing Lord Hugh by the collar of his shirt and physically hoisting him off of her.

She took in large deep gulps of air as tears streamed down her face. Relief came, replacing the trepidation and anger, leaving her trembling.

"I believe it is time for you to go home, Lord Hugh," Richard growled. "You've clearly had too much to drink."

"Not at all," Lord Hugh replied with a chuckle, releasing himself from Richard's grip and straightening his clothing. "Methinks the lady doth protest too much."

Georgiana watched in silence, attempting to regain her composure.

Lord Hugh continued speaking, his mouth curled in a smirk. "It is of little consequence to me if she will not favour me with a kiss. Soon we will be married and, as her husband, I will be entitled to as many kisses I should wish for."

Georgiana watched as the blood drained from Richard's face.

"Married?" his voice no louder than a whisper.

"No!" Georgiana shook her head vehemently.

"Oh, yes," Lord Hugh countered arrogantly. "I have made up my mind, you see." His eyes bored into Georgiana's. "We shall be married."

The words hung heavily in the air as he stomped out of the room. He called to his sister. "Come on, Fran. It is time we departed." The edge in his voice disappeared. "Lady Matlock, I thank you for your hospitality, but we must away."

While Lord Hugh and Lady Francesca prepared to leave, Georgiana and Richard stood immobile staring at each other, neither of them quite believing what they had just witnessed.

Nineteen

The events following Lord Hugh's departure were a haze to Georgiana. She remembered saying good night to some of the guests and being teased by Aunt Henrietta about Lord Hugh and what the older woman termed Georgiana's partiality. The only thing that stood out and was burned into her memory was Richard's face and the look in his eyes when he walked in on her in Lord Hugh's arms.

She barely slept a wink that night. She paced up and down until she was too tired to continue, then wept into her pillow until dawn.

She must have slept after that because she woke to the sound of Meg drawing the curtains and bringing her some tea. She rolled over as the maid greeted her. The last thing she wanted was for her to see her puffy eyes and ask uncomfortable questions. Thankfully, Meg took the grunt to mean her mistress wanted more sleep and left her alone.

Georgiana decided to skip breakfast and stay in bed late. That night was the charity Christmas ball that Aunt Henrietta wanted to attend. She knew there was no getting out of it and that Lord Hugh would no doubt be there as well.

As she drifted in and out of sleep, she thought of one hundred and one excuses to get out of going. She was fully aware that none of them would work. When her aunt was determined, there was no gainsaying her.

Around noon, unaware that Meg had come in and out of the room repeatedly, Georgiana rose, dressed in the pale-yellow muslin Meg had laid out, and made her way downstairs to the drawing room.

She was so tired. She knew there were bags under her eyes. As she opened the door to the drawing room, she braced herself for the onslaught of comments from her aunt.

The room was empty.

"Might I help you, Miss?"

Georgiana jumped at Hobbs' voice and spun around. "Where is everyone?"

Hobbs replied in his slow, sedate way, "Colonel Fitzwilliam has taken Lady Matlock out in the carriage. I believe she needs some new gloves for this evening's charity ball, Miss."

"Oh," she deflated, relieved to not have to defend herself quite yet. "Did they say when they would be back?"

"They did not." When she continued to gaze at him expectantly, he added, "I expect they will be back in time for tea, Miss."

"Good. Thank you, Hobbs." Georgiana turned around and surveyed the empty room, which no longer felt welcoming without its family.

"Would you perhaps like something to eat, Miss?"

Georgiana turned back, pleased Hobbs had not left her alone. "I would. Thank you."

"If you would make your way to the breakfast room, I shall have something hot prepared for you immediately."

Georgiana smiled for possibly the first time that day. She ambled her way through the house towards the breakfast room at the back, her mind securely fixated upon the goings-on of the previous night. She hesitated outside the door to the dining room, her mind taunting her with visions of the previous night.

She waited patiently until the table was set and then sat down to eat. Her stomach growled as she laid eyes on the devilled eggs, toast, poached salmon, and pot of tea. The food was like honey on her lips and, tucking in, she discovered she was far more ravenous than she previously thought.

As she ate, she stared out through the French doors into the garden, watching a few snowflakes drift to the ground. By the time she finished, there was a light dusting of snow covering everything. Part of her wished it was snowing so heavily they could not go out that night.

As Georgina crossed the hallway heading to her uncle's study, having decided to read until Richard and Aunt Henrietta returned, they arrived home.

"Oh, my dear!" Aunt Henrietta declared as she burst through the doors. "I do not believe I have ever known London to be this cold!" She made a commotion of taking off her coat, bonnet, removing her muff, and slipping from her outdoor shoes. "I bought you a little gift," she grinned, signalling to the servant carrying the boxes to follow her into the drawing room.

Georgiana trailed closely behind.

"The shops are simply heaving with people," Aunt Henrietta informed her, warming herself before the fire. "Everyone, it seems, had the silly idea to leave it until the last minute to go shopping for any items they need for tonight's ball." She shook her head in disbelief.

"Surely not everyone is going to the same ball, Mama." Richard strode into the room, poured his mother a glass of sherry, handed it to her, and returned to the drinks table. "Can I get you something?" he asked Georgiana without looking her in her direction.

"No, thank you," she replied.

Her voice was so small, he clearly did not hear her. He poured another glass of sherry, along with a single finger of whiskey for himself, and brought it to her. Part of her was relieved when he did not sit down on the same settee but chose instead to be seated on the opposite side of the room.

Aunt Henrietta was chatting away, but Georgiana heard nary a word. Her full attention was on Richard. They hadn't talked since he burst in on her and Lord Hugh the night before. She wanted to defend herself, to explain to him that it was not what he thought. She chewed the inside of her cheek. *I wonder what he does think was going on last night.* The very thought that he was thinking ill of her churned her stomach, and she regretted eating lunch.

"Kid gloves, Georgiana!"

Georgiana snapped out of her reverie to see Aunt Henrietta waving a pair of gloves at her. Her grin told Georgiana they were meant for her. She leant forward and took them. They were the softest pair of kid leather she'd ever held in her hands. They were ivory with delicate pale blue stitching and leaf motif on the wrist. "How beautiful!" she exclaimed.

"I knew the moment I saw them that they were perfect for you. Such pretty little stitching, don't you think?"

"Yes, I do. Thank you, Aunt." Georgiana ran her fingers along the stitching. It was delicate work.

"I think we should all meet down here for tea and crumpets an hour before we depart. What say you, Richard?" Aunt Henrietta asked while fiddling with the other boxes.

"I think that is a splendid idea, Mama. There will likely be far more people than usual in the assembly rooms. I doubt very much we will be able to get in to eat anything, and the last thing I want is you overheated." Richard watched his mother.

Georgiana continued to observe him while feigning interest in her gloves. They were exquisite indeed, but her mind was occupied. She was racked with guilt and shame. She realised full well she had done nothing wrong, but all the same, she could not shake the sense of culpability.

"Oh, absolutely!" Aunt Henrietta threw her hands up in the air. "As much as I enjoy a ball, there's nothing worse than going to one with too many people in attendance." She picked up another smaller box and brought it to Georgiana. "It's a ticketed event, after all, so why they sell far too many tickets, I do not know."

"It is for charity. Perhaps that is the reason," Richard replied diplomatically.

"Well, it is most inconvenient," Aunt Henrietta snapped back. She turned and addressed Georgiana. "This too is for you, my dear."

Georgiana was astonished at her aunt's generosity. She placed her glass on the table before her and took the box in her hands. Prizing off the lid, Georgiana discovered an exquisite pearl headdress inside. "My goodness!" she gasped.

"I thought you'd like it. Isn't it beautiful?" Aunt Henrietta cooed.

Georgiana's eyes danced. "It's so pretty."

Aunt Henrietta sat down beside her. "I bought us each a couple of new pairs of stockings as well," she lowered her voice to a rasping whisper, "but we shan't take those out of the box in front of Richard, shall we?"

Georgiana reddened. "No."

Stretching out her hand, Aunt Henrietta fondled the pearl headdress as Georgiana admired it. "You can either wear it tonight or save it for a special occasion. Perhaps for your engagement party," she chuckled with delight, her eyes glistening with amusement.

Georgiana's hot cheeks suddenly felt stone cold, as the blood drained from her face.

"Come now, Georgiana!" Aunt Henrietta continued to chuckle. "Don't be missish! You and Lord Hugh were alone last night. Don't try to tell me there is no understanding between the pair of you."

Georgiana shook her head, her mouth falling open. "No, there isn't, Aunt. I assure you."

"Nonsense!" Aunt Henrietta pursed her lips together and folded her arms across her chest. "I do not understand this fashion for secret engagements. It is clear there is a partiality on his side at least, and," she twisted and leant her facing close to Georgiana's, "unless my eyes have greatly deceived me, I also detect a partiality on your side."

Georgiana's eyes darted, looking pleadingly to Richard, hoping that he would come to her defence while, deep inside, the voice of guilt and shame shouted louder that he would not.

"There's no point in denying it. You were alone together, and I would not allow that sort of comportment in my house if I did not suspect you were engaged," Aunt Henrietta scolded.

Tears welled in Georgiana's eyes. *I am not engaged to Lord Hugh and neither will I ever be.*

"Perhaps we should leave well alone, Mama. Unless Georgiana decides to divulge what happened between her and

Lord Hugh last night, we have only conjecture on our side." Richard did not even look at her.

"Young people today!" Aunt Henrietta clicked her tongue on the roof of her mouth. "I do not know what they are about. Such silly dalliances all the time, fancying themselves in love hither and thither. In my day such silly foolhardiness would be a disgrace." She rounded on Georgiana again. "You make up your mind, young miss. Either you are engaged to be married to Lord Hugh DeVere, or you are not."

Georgiana found her voice, her skin cold and clammy. "I am not."

Aunt Henrietta's eyes bulged out of their sockets. "Then you will promise me that you will never speak to him alone and unchaperoned."

Georgiana nodded rapidly and swallowed hard, fighting back the tears. "I promise."

"Good. I will not have scandal in this house, do you hear?" She wagged a finger in her face.

Aunt Henrietta rose, gathered up her boxes, and stormed out of the room. With trembling fingers Georgiana picked up the sherry glass and drank all of it in one go. When she finally found the courage to look up again, she discovered Richard watching her.

"Was that the truth?" His voice had a bitter edge to it.

Georgiana's eyes welled. "Yes," she replied, scarcely louder than a whisper.

Richard huffed. He gulped back his whiskey and slammed the glass on the ornate walnut inlaid table. "His hands were all over you," he growled, his voice scaring her.

Her heart constricted, and she screwed up her face in hurt. "It was not at my bidding," she replied as the tears spilled out of her eyes, down her cheeks, and landed on her dress.

Richard's expression softened. "Forgive me."

Twenty

Richard awaited the ladies in the drawing room, resisting the urge to smoke a cigar. The smell of the smoke on his clothes would not make him a pleasant dancing partner. His intention was to keep Georgiana within his sight all night long if need be.

Something about her tears and countenance earlier told him she was telling the truth and hurting deeply. It wasn't a long leap of logic to know that the blame would lie entirely at Lord Hugh's feet.

When she descended the stairs, dressed in the most beautiful ivory silk gown, her head adorned with the pearl headdress his mother had gifted her, Georgiana took his breath away. The smile she wore as their eyes connected was for him and him alone. His heart swelled in his chest. Every day confirmed, beyond a shadow of a doubt, that he was falling in love with his cousin. He had no idea what Fitzwilliam Darcy would say, or his mother for that matter. But, in the first flush of love, he cared not what anyone said, apart from Georgiana herself.

He held out his hand and sighed gently as she took it. "You look stunningly beautiful this evening."

She repaid his compliment by blushing a deep crimson. "Thank you, Richard." She pointed to her expertly coiffed hair. "I am wearing the headdress, you see?"

"Indeed, I did see. It looks well on you. My mother was right. It is a perfect adornment for your silken curls."

Not far behind her, his mother appeared at the top of the stairs, and once he had greeted and kissed her on the cheek, the party of three departed for the charity Christmas ball.

The night was bitterly cold, and their carriage contained two heated bricks to stave off the chill, though it was not enough to prevent their breath fogging up the interior as they rode along. Concerned that the two women would be warm enough, Richard quickly surveyed their attire. Satisfied that the thick fur cloaks they wore were sufficient for the journey, he relaxed a little. Gazing out of the window, the stars twinkled back at him. "It looks like there will be a hard frost tonight."

"It is good, then, that we shall be going from carriage to assembly room and back to the carriage again," his mother replied, snuggling up a little closer to Georgiana.

"A little dancing will warm us up, I daresay," Georgiana added.

"Unfortunately, I am not in a mind to dance," the older woman replied. "I believe my dancing days are long gone."

Richard smiled lovingly at his mother. "Do not say such things, Mother. You are not yet past it, as they say. If you had a mind to dance, you would cut a fine jig."

"Oh, fie!" Lady Matlock flapped her hand at her son.

Chuckling, Richard replied, "I remember you used to be one of the finest dancers I've ever seen, Mama."

She made a noise that sounded like a cross between shh and pff.

He smiled at her indulgently. "If you change your mind, Mama, I would be more than willing to indulge you in a turn around the room."

She eyed him suspiciously. "You shall do no such thing," her eyes narrowed.

He splayed his hands before him. "The offer is there and shall not be rescinded, Mama."

He watched with satisfaction as she inclined her head towards Georgiana and whispered, "He is so good to me."

Richard's breath caught in his throat as Georgiana looked directly at him, and straight into his soul. "He is good to us both."

He could not respond. There was nothing to say, or at least there was nothing in his mind to say. He tried to think rationally. Georgiana was merely expressing gratitude, but a shred of hope inside him dared to believe it was more than that. Much more.

* * *

Georgiana stepped out onto the pavement, the shock of the chill night catching her breath. “Oh! So cold!” she exclaimed, hearing others mirroring her sentiments around her.

Feeling Richard’s hand on her elbow, Georgiana allowed herself to be manoeuvred across the street, up the steps, and into the assembly room. Immediately the heat and noise of the crowd inside hit them.

“Oh, good!” Aunt Henrietta breathed in her ear. “I think this is the first time in years I’ve ever been glad of a mass of people.”

Richard steered them through the throng. Looking ahead of them, Georgiana spied Alex with Miss Hawkins in conversation with Louis. Knowing their direction, she aided Richard in pushing through the revellers.

“What ho!” Louis called out in greeting upon seeing them. “Lady Matlock,” he bowed, “what a pleasure it is to see you again this evening.”

Aunt Henrietta inclined her head. She was not one for curtseying. “Young man,” she tapped him on the shoulder with her fan, “do you see anywhere a person of my great age might be seated and still be able to watch the dancers?”

Georgiana watched on as Louis looked about him. “I shall see what I can do,” he replied, bowing his head, then turning and disappearing into the crowd.

Georgiana curtsied to Alex and Rebecca. “Good evening.”

Rebecca took hold of her hands. “Oh, I am so glad you are both here.” She blew out a long breath as though she had been holding it. "Apart from Alex and Louis, I am not acquainted with anyone here, I don't think."

"Fear not, Miss Hawkins," Richard soothed her. "Between the three of us, you will have plenty of gentlemen to dance with."

She giggled with excitement, and Georgiana found herself liking Rebecca even more.

"And if Alex does not mind," Richard looked pointedly at his friend, "I would like to take this opportunity of soliciting your hand for the second dance."

"I have no objections whatsoever," Alex beamed down at his intended, who was more than a head shorter than he was. He then caught Georgiana's eye. "If they are to dance the second dance together, shall we not dance it ourselves?"

Georgiana decided she liked Alex. He was affable, and she was comfortable in his presence. "Nothing would please me more," she replied.

Louis returned, Georgiana suspected having displaced one or two patrons of the assembly rooms, and escorted Aunt Henrietta across the room where he sat down with her and started conversation.

Georgiana squinted at them across the room. "Does Louis know Aunt Henrietta well? They seem to be deep into conversation already."

Richard chuckled close to her ear, sending warm liquid shiver down her spine. "I was at school with Louis, Alex, and George. So Mama knows them all rather well and has done since we were lads." He craned his neck to see over the heads of those nearest them. “Speaking of George, where is the old devil?”

“Where do you think he is?” Alex drawled. “At the gaming tables as usual.”

“He never was one for dancing, was he?” Richard laughed, sharing a private joke between himself and his friend.

“No, not at all! Two left feet!” Alex threw his head back and laughed. He turned to his fiancée and explained, “To own the truth, my dear, I would pity any woman who had the misfortune of dancing with George Branford. Not only does he have two left feet, but she would find her own flattened and bruised all the way up the shins, no doubt.”

Both Georgiana and Rebecca winced at the same time.

Alex continued, “Believe me, it is better all round if George remains at the gaming tables.”

Richard nodded vehemently. “Undeniably. He seems to have more than his fair share of luck in that arena.”

“In fact,” Alex added, “he more than doubles his ample income every year because of how lucky he is gambling.”

Georgiana inhaled. “Really?” She looked up at Richard for confirmation.

He nodded. “Really. He is that good.”

Soon after, strains of music could be heard from further down the ballroom and couples started to move about, make space, and pair up.

“May I?” Richard held out his hand for Georgiana to take.

A broad grin spread across her face. There was nothing that would please her more than to remain by Richard’s side all evening long. If she could possibly avoid it, she would not dance with Lord Hugh ever again for the whole course of her life. She thanked Heaven that her stay in London was finite.

As she reached out and took her cousin's hand, she prayed earnestly that neither Lord Hugh nor his sister Lady Francesca were present.

To begin with they danced *A Fig for Bonaparte,* which enabled them to stay as a foursome. Georgiana slowly pushed all thoughts of Lord Hugh from her mind and unwound. The next was *The Lady's Joy,* in which another couple joined them. It was one of Georgiana's favourite dances as they danced in a circle for some of it. During that second jig, she discovered Alex was also a talented dancer, like her cousin Richard.

They then danced a cotillion, *La Liberté,* where their party of three couples was joined by another. Georgiana's throat went dry upon spying Lord Hugh and his sister, Lady Francesca. She did her utmost to plant a smile on her face and curtsey to the siblings, while all the joy she had begun to feel fled from her heart.

As she took her place, Richard whispered in her ear, "Stay close by me."

Georgiana nodded, full of gratitude for those four simple words. "I have every intention of doing precisely that."

She saw satisfaction on Richard's face, and her sensation of being safe with him increased.

La Liberté, a dance Georgiana usually adored, lost something of its appeal. Thankfully, the steps were complicated enough for her to have to concentrate on what she was doing. Otherwise, she knew Lord Hugh would take all her attention.

She put her mind and energy into the dance, keeping her eyes on Richard alone; and by the time the dance ended, she could say that she was enjoying herself again.

As soon as the music ended and the couples applauded the octet of musicians, Richard hastily whisked her away to the side. He found an empty seat swiftly enough, and Alex and Rebecca joined them.

"I shall procure some refreshments," Richard bowed to the ladies. As he turned away, he leant in close and whispered, "Whatever you do, do not agree to dance with him."

As she watched his back retreat from view, Georgiana wondered why he was so adamant. For certain, she had no intention of dancing with Lord Hugh after his deplorable behaviour at the dinner party, and she began to suspect that Richard knew more about him than he was letting on. Her eyes narrowed. She wondered what it was when her train of thought was broken by the arrival of Lord Hugh and his sister.

"Deuce it all!" Lord Hugh exclaimed, drawing all attention to himself. "This is the busiest I've ever seen this place!"

Georgiana did not reply, but he was right; this assembly hall was far busier than the previous time they were there.

"We've danced three dances already, and I have not yet had the opportunity or pleasure of dancing with my beloved Georgiana," he sulked.

Georgiana paled and wished the floor would open up and swallow her.

To her great relief, Alex stepped in. "Miss Darcy has been happily engaged with her cousin. A fine couple they make when dancing, don't you think?"

Georgiana watched Lord Hugh's colour rise as Alex baited him.

"All the same," he turned steely eyes upon her, "I am more than a little offended that she did not dance with me first."

Alex chuckled forcedly, doing his level best to defuse the situation that was growing increasingly tense. "I can understand your being desirous of dancing with her. Miss Darcy is a most excellent dancer. I believe etiquette would dictate that she dance the first with her cousin, would it not?"

"And slight me?" Lord Hugh bawled, clearly affronted. A vein in the side of his neck stuck out.

"I fail to see why you would be slighted, Lord Hugh." Alex's tone changed dramatically, and he stepped forward. "After all, you are not promised in marriage to each other. Therefore, as far as I can tell, Miss Darcy is free to dance with whomever she chooses."

Lord Hugh's nostrils flared. He ground his teeth together and looked on the verge of saying something spiteful when Richard returned with a tray containing four glasses in his hands.

"Here you are Miss Hawkins, Georgiana, Alex," he said, deliberately ignoring Lord Hugh and his sister, and going so far as to turn his back on them.

Georgiana took one of the glasses of fruit punch and passed it to Rebecca. Alex leant past and took one for himself, leaving the remaining two for her and Richard. Despite knowing the punch was well diluted, Georgiana sipped it carefully, aware of her thirst and the likelihood of the alcohol going straight to her head. She caught Richard's eye. "Thank you," she mouthed.

Lord Hugh huffed, and Georgiana watched him out of the corner of her eye while she fixed on her fruit punch. He most certainly looked out of sorts. His sister, on the other hand, was doing her best to jiggle from foot to foot in, what Georgiana thought, was the vain hope of catching Richard's eye.

It did not take long before she gave up trying and blurted out, "I would like some of that fruit punch. It looks mightily tempting."

If Georgiana was not mistaken, Lady Francesca even stamped her foot. The four in her group remained silent, their eyes fixed on anything but Lady Francesca, until Lord Hugh groaned.

"For goodness sake! I suppose I shall have to go and get you a drink myself, seeing as nobody else will do it for you." He stomped off glaring at the back of Richard's head. Richard, however, was unaffected by his outburst.

"I wonder if there's any chance of my dancing again tonight..." Lady Francesca grouched.

Georgiana held a groan within her until it subsided. She watched as Richard and Alex stared at each other. Clearly, their long-standing friendship had given them an understanding of each other that extended to communicating with just one look.

"I will dance with you if my fiancée will release me," Alex mumbled. "We can't have you without a dance partner if Lord Hugh is not inclined."

She looked disappointed and dragged her eyes away from Richard's face to address Alex. "Oh, he is inclined to dance, just not with me." She looked pointedly at Georgiana, and her eyes threw daggers. "Unfortunately, the young lady with whom he wishes to dance has been occupied thus far." The pout deepened, and she leant ever so slightly forward as though she was speaking only to Georgiana. "Let this be a warning to you, Miss Darcy, my brother does not take kindly to being insulted or slighted by women."

Georgiana's mouth fell open and her eyes opened as wide as saucers. Irritation bottled up inside her and bubbled over. "I beg your pardon, but I know nothing of the slight or insult to which you and your brother have both referred," she snapped. "I have come here to dance with my cousin. I have no other prior arrangements to dance with any other gentleman, excepting Mr Salisbury. Therefore, I am perfectly at liberty to dance with whomever I choose."

She gripped the punch cup with both hands to stop the trembling from sloshing the liquid out and over her silk dress. Her eyes flicked upwards and she caught amusement playing on Richard's mouth.

"What say you, Rebecca dearest?" Alex asked as though the altercation between Lady Francesca and Georgiana had never taken place.

Rebecca smiled up at her betrothed and laid her tiny hand upon his arm. "I have no objections whatsoever to your dancing with Lady Francesca." She turned to the woman they discussed. "Of course you must have someone to dance with. It would be a crying shame if someone so elegant had to sit out any of tonight's dances."

Georgiana watched in amusement as Rebecca touched and toyed with Lady Francesca's ego. If there was one thing that could break through her irritation and anger at Georgiana, it was being flattered.

"Why, my dear Miss Hawkins, what a nice thing to say." She flattened her hand across her chest and batted her eyelids. "I must admit that I am enormously fond of dancing."

Isn't everyone? Georgiana thought bitterly as she drank to the bottom of her cup.

"Splendid!" Alex declared. "That's settled."

The current dance ended. Alex led Lady Francesca away. Richard stepped a little closer to Georgiana. She grinned and took hold of his arm, knowing instinctively what he intended. She was filled with the greatest excitement as he led her towards the dance floor again.

As they took their places, Georgiana peeked back to see if Rebecca had found somewhere to sit. She spied her friend and at the same time saw Lord Hugh return with two glasses of punch. His head was so red, Georgiana thought it might burst with rage.

The refrain continued to play, and Georgiana counted out the beats before she would take a first step. It wasn't until she passed behind Richard that she was able to view Rebecca again. It seemed she was being her friendly self and endeavouring to engage Lord Hugh in conversation. Regrettably, he was clearly in no mood for a tête-à-tête.

Georgiana kept an eye on Rebecca. Anger boiled in her belly once again, for, if she was not mistaken, she could have sworn Lord Hugh looked down upon Rebecca, his lip curled in disgust.

Georgiana glared at Richard and nodded back towards Rebecca. The pair turned about in their set and just saw Lord Hugh's back as he pushed and shoved his way through the crowd, away from Rebecca.

Georgiana felt helpless. It would not do to rush from the dance floor to her friend's aid. All eyes would be upon her if she did so. The last thing Georgiana wanted was to draw attention to herself.

She pleaded with Richard when he was within earshot again. "We must do something. We cannot leave poor Rebecca sitting there alone. Goodness knows how Lord Hugh may have insulted her."

Georgiana smiled kindly at the next man in the set as they do-si-doed around each other.

"I cannot believe he did not even think to either stay there and keep her company or to ask if she wanted to dance," she hissed at Richard.

"I can."

There it was again. Georgiana frowned. That same tone which suggested that Richard knew more about Lord Hugh than she could imagine. There was something deeper than dislike within it. There was a hatred and loathing to his tone.

"We will be at the end of the line, closest to Rebecca in a moment." Georgiana brushed past his arm. "I shall fetch her, and she can take my place."

"What?" Richard asked, the hatred in his voice gone and replaced instantly with something akin to panic. "What about Lord Hugh?"

"He stormed off, didn't he?" Georgiana set her chin. "I shall seek out Aunt Henrietta. I shall be perfectly safe, I assure you."

His eyes bored into hers, and she felt the now familiar jolt of lightning pass through her body, warming her instantly and making her more than a little giddy.

She giggled as she shot out of place, grabbed Rebecca by the hands, and dragged her into the dance. She laughed heartily as her friend looked confused by what was going on. As she skipped past on her way to sit with her aunt, she sing-songed, "Dance, Rebecca! Dance!"

* * *

Richard enjoyed his short but sweet dance with Rebecca. *Alex is one lucky man to have found such a treasure. I am happy for him.*

She wasn't quite the dancer Georgiana was. She lacked a certain elegance that only Georgiana had. He laughed at himself. *I believe I'm a little bit biased there.* However, she was fun and sprightly, and her conversation was intelligent and informed. He vowed if ever he had the opportunity to dance with Rebecca again, he most undoubtedly would not hesitate to take it.

When the music stopped, he wrapped Rebecca's arm around his own and smiled down at her. They were out of breath from their exertions, but he noticed the colour in her cheeks made her even prettier.

He led her through the throng, carefully picking out a path in which she would not get an elbow in the face which, he realised to his dismay, was a real and present danger of being so petite.

They joined his mother and Georgiana. A minute or two later Alex arrived.

"Did you lose Lady Francesca along the way?" Rebecca asked, turning around and scanning the room.

Alex chuckled. "I would never be so careless." He rubbed the back of his neck. "No, as soon as the dance finished, there was an entire queue of gentlemen waiting to dance with her." He glanced askance at Richard. "Who am I to stand in their way?"

Rebecca declared she would like to sit out the next dance with Georgiana, giving Richard and Alex the opportunity to seek out their friend George.

The room in which the card tables were set up was towards the back of the building. The farther they got away from the ballroom, the easier it was to walk and find their path. The air was less stifling as well.

They found George in the farthest corner, surrounded by a cloud of blue cigar smoke, chuckling to himself as he laid down a winning hand.

"The lucky so-and-so has won again!" Alex whispered to Richard.

"Did you ever doubt it?" Richard replied, chuckling.

George looked up at them, his eyes glistening with his success. He pulled the cigar from his mouth. "I wondered when you two would turn up."

The three men he had been playing against got up and left, grumbling.

"Sore losers. They're everywhere."

Richard and Alex sat down at the table and helped George count his winnings.

"Can you blame them?" Richard asked.

"I play fairly and honestly. They've had every opportunity to beat me." George guffawed and shoved the cigar back into his mouth.

Once all the winnings were counted, Richard whistled long and low. "Three hundred and forty pounds," he muttered under his breath. "You made that all in one night?"

"Yup!" George was clearly pleased with himself and looked like the cat who had got the cream. "I think I'll call it a night, though."

He nodded to one or two of the other tables, and Richard and Alex furtively surveyed the remainder.

"It appears I'm making myself quite a number of enemies," he chuckled, shaking his head. "Methinks I've exhausted my avenue of income tonight."

"Not to mention the fact this is supposed to be a *charity* ball," Alex whispered in response.

"I paid for my ticket!" George flicked the ash off the end of his cigar onto the floor. "What more do they want?"

Richard carefully laid his hands over the stack of notes on the table and pushed them towards his friend. "Perhaps it would be politic and generous of you to make a sizeable donation." He glanced around the room one more time. "It might go some way to turning the tide of opinion that is currently against you."

George eyeballed him for a moment, sucking hard on his cigar, making the end light up a deep, dark reddish orange. "Always the diplomat, eh, Richard?" After a moment, George nodded in agreement. "You are right, though. I will donate, and I jolly well will make sure this lot see me doing it."

As one of the charity volunteers passed by with a collection pail, George made a show of standing up, counting out one hundred pounds, and making sure everyone in the room saw him putting it into the bucket.

He sat back down at the table and stubbed out the balance of his cigar into the ashtray. "So how's your evening going?"

Twenty-one

Feeling refreshed, Georgiana was ready to dance again and hoped Richard would return soon. Instead, the re-emergence of one particular gentleman made her heart sink.

"Miss Darcy," Lord Hugh bowed low before her.

Georgiana swallowed but had no desire to smile.

"I wonder if you might give me the pleasure, and honour, of dancing with me?" he asked, his voice curt and words clipped.

Nervously, Georgiana looked to Aunt Henrietta for help. Unfortunately, her aunt merely nodded, her expression declaring, "Go on, then!!"

Georgiana's spirits plummeted. She had promised herself and Richard that she would never dance with Lord Hugh again, and yet here she was faced with a dilemma. If she refused him, he might very well cause another scene or, worse still, force himself upon her again. Yet there was one opportunity that dancing with him afforded her—the chance to speak with him and set the record straight between them.

Georgiana squared her jaw, bracing herself for close contact with the man she was now beginning to despise. "Very well," she replied brusquely. "Just this once, then."

Anger flickered in his eyes, and Georgiana knew full well that he was barely controlling it. He held out his hand and Georgiana took it, resting hers so lightly upon it, she gave only the appearance of holding his hand.

Lord Hugh, regrettably, closed his fingers around hers and gripped her so tightly she yelped in pain.

"That hurts!" She glowered at him.

He did not respond. Instead, he pulled her to the dance floor where a cotillion had just begun.

They took their places and Georgiana found she could not bear to even look at him. Nevertheless, Lord Hugh initiated conversation. Georgiana had to respond; otherwise, she might never have another occasion to do so.

"I must say you have treated me despicably, Miss Darcy."

Georgiana's head snapped around, her eyes throwing daggers at him. "I have treated you despicably?"

"Indeed, you have." The look of superiority on his face turned Georgiana stomach. "You cannot deny there was something between us. In fact, there is still something between us, I daresay."

Georgiana did not rise to the bait but continued to dance.

"We are in love, Georgiana."

Inwardly, Georgiana groaned. *He is using my Christian name again. I wish he wouldn't.* She regretted giving him permission to do so. It was an intimacy she no longer wanted.

"We had an understanding, did we not?"

Georgiana's jaw dropped open. "We most certainly did not, Lord Hugh!"

She watched as he rolled his eyes and tilted his head backwards, groaning as though in pain. The two couples in their set watched them closely. Georgiana ignored their attention but knew there was nothing society liked more than a good scandal and a jolly good bit of gossip about it.

"Oh, dearest Georgiana! How could you be so callous to a fellow?" He raised his voice so the other couples could hear.

She wanted to scream at him to stop but knew he wouldn't. She debated walking away from the dance but, alas, that would add gravitas to his words.

"We had an understanding, and you know it," he hissed, passing close to her ear. "Now you've gone cold on me."

Georgiana did her level best to concentrate on the steps of the dance, but his words pounded in her ears.

"I do not take kindly to being jilted, Georgiana."

Georgiana stopped dancing causing two of the others in their set to crash into her. She glared at Lord Hugh, her fists clenched by her side. "There is no understanding between us and there never was. It is all a flight of fancy on your part. We are not engaged to be married, and I have most certainly not jilted you, Lord Hugh. Your imagination has run away with you, and this must stop here and now."

She did not wait to hear his reply. She turned on her heel and marched out of the room. She did not stop walking, shoving her way past the patrons, until she reached the front door. She burst through it and clung on to the stone balustrade for dear life. She willed her lungs to take in air. She shook from head to foot with anger, and tears poured down her cheeks. "What a dreadful odious man!" she sobbed.

* * *

Upon his return from the gaming room with Alex and George, Richard made a beeline for his mother. They found her and Rebecca sitting together, deep in conversation.

His mother looked up at him, evidently pleased to see him. "There you are, Richard! Dear Miss Hawkins and I had just begun to think we were deserted by our menfolk."

Richard bowed. "Forgive me, Mama. I went in search of George here," he turned to the side indicating his friend. "I found him at the gaming tables, raising funds for the charity, no less."

"Oh, how delightful!" She clapped her hands together with glee, turning her attention to George. "And might I enquire how much you raised?"

George puffed out his chest and stuck his thumbs into the pockets of his waistcoat. "Aye, ma'am, you may. I raised no less than one hundred pounds for the benevolence fund."

"That is wonderful!" Both she and Rebecca seemed delighted.

Alex led his fiancée away to dance once again, and Richard looked about him for Georgiana while George took a seat next to Richard's mother.

"Mama, where is Georgiana?" he asked.

"She's dancing, isn't she?" Lady Matlock replied, craning her head to see past the revellers to the dance floor.

"Not that I can see," Richard replied, growing concerned. "With whom was she dancing?" he asked, fearing he already knew the answer to that question.

"Why, with Lord Hugh, of course!" His mother replied as though that were obvious. "They are sweethearts after all, are they not?"

Richard spun around and glared pointedly at his mother. She shrunk away from his glare. "No, Mother. They most certainly are not sweethearts. Be under no illusion on that score."

His mother opened and closed her mouth repeatedly. "But, I..."

"I know what you thought, Mama. And I most certainly know what Lord Hugh has led us to believe is true. But there is no understanding between them, they are not sweethearts, and Georgiana most certainly has no intention of marrying him." Richard was not entirely sure. Everything he said he had surmised from her looks and tears the day before.

"We are deceived?" She looked scandalised.

"Indeed, we are." Richard returned to looking for his cousin. With every passing second, he grew increasingly concerned for her safety. He could not see either of them amongst the dancers. *Oh, dear God! Where could they possibly be?*

Richard was not naïve. He was a man of the world. He served in His Majesty's army for long enough to know the dangers that could befall a young innocent girl under the spell of a blackguard. He also knew first-hand what Lord Hugh was capable of. In his mind he saw Margaret Ainsworth's tearstained face, her little baby in her arms. A barely constrained anger built up inside him. If there was anything that years of service had taught Richard, it was to abhor and to fight against injustice wherever he found it.

He lifted his head and beheld the ornately plastered ceiling. He knew this building well. He had been to countless balls and soirées here. He knew there were rooms above stairs. And he was well aware of what went on behind those closed doors.

His throat went dry.

He looked down at his mother momentarily. "Will you be all right here if I go off and look for her?"

His mother sat staring at him, her hands on her chest, and her face pale with worry. "Please do go and search for her. Bring her back." She groaned. "Oh, that poor dear girl. What must she think of me for believing she was enamoured of him!" Her bottom lip trembled. "I scolded her something fierce, didn't I?"

Richard's expression softened. "Do not worry yourself, Mama. We both believed there was an understanding between them, did we not?"

Lady Matlock nodded. "I was so excited to think that she was in love that I did not even stop to think whether it was true or not." She shook her head from side to side, closing her eyes. "I should have known. No one can fall in love that quickly. Attraction comes first; love comes after."

Richard leant forward and kissed his mother on the cheek. "I'm certain they have merely gone for refreshments. I shall be back presently." He smiled, turned around, and made his way across the anteroom. His destination was the staircase in the grand entrance hall.

He did not believe that Georgiana was the kind of girl to so easily fall prey to the lusts of a hot-blooded male. However, he did most certainly believe Lord Hugh was capable of any kind of deception, and, after what he saw the previous night, he believed him capable of forcing himself on her.

His blood ran cold as he took the stairs two at a time, knowing that he must open as many doors as he could and peer inside. He had seen many bloody sites on the battlefield—men with limbs blown off and those even worse, the unrecognisable—but he did not know if he possessed the stomach to see what he suspected lay waiting for him inside those upstairs rooms. Especially not if Georgiana was involved.

Richard marched along the landing hallway, his footsteps muffled in the carpet runner. He tried doorknob after doorknob, but they were locked. His panic beginning to rise, he redoubled his efforts, bursting through a door he was surprised to find unlocked.

The shouts and cheers from within caused him to recoil. The mass of heaving bodies on the bed, rugs, and other furniture sent him reeling backwards. He slammed the door closed again. Clearly, no one was policing the event. The women inside looked to him to be ladies of the night.

He took a deep breath and dashed on to the next one.

Every door he opened, he came up with a blank. Georgiana and Lord Hugh were nowhere to be seen. Part of him hoped they were indeed below stairs taking refreshments somewhere; most of him still believed that behind one of the remaining doors, he would find Lord Hugh. He paused, bracing himself against the doorframe. His stomach flipped over, and he thought he would vomit. His affection for Georgiana had grown exponentially recently, and the very thought of her in Lord Hughes arms repulsed him. He had no idea whatsoever whether she would ever come to love him as dearly as he was beginning to love her, but he would never, ever wish for her to wind up with the same fate as Margaret Ainsworth.

That reflection buoyed him up. He tried the last remaining few door handles, but it was to no avail. They too were locked.

Richard stood staring at the final door. If Lord Hugh was not behind this door with Georgiana, then perhaps she was safe. He clung on to that as he reached for the knob.

Turning it slowly, he heard it click, and then he pushed it.

Richard averted his eyes at the sight of the young woman's garter holding up her stocking. A gentleman stood between her thighs, his breeches around his ankles.

Richard's throat clamped shut. His knees weakened beneath him. He clutched the door to hold himself up.

The woman saw him first. She squealed with delight. "'Ello darlin' want to join in, do ya?" she cackled at him. "It'll be extra!"

Richard turned to leave, sickened at the sight, but the sound of the gentleman's voice bellowing at him to get out stopped him in his tracks, freezing his blood. It was Lord Hugh.

When he was able to look in their direction, and sufficiently in control of his emotions, he glowered at Lord Hugh long enough for the man to see the anger burning within his eyes.

"Are you deaf? I said get out!" Lord Hugh hollered.

Richard wasn't listening. He had one thing on his mind. "Where's Georgiana?" he bellowed back.

Lord Hugh shrugged. "How the hell should I know?" he spat. "She ran off and left me."

Lord Hugh's words filled Richard with a twisted sort of satisfaction. He left, slamming the door behind him. As he did so, Lord Hugh yelled, "Trust me, she won't get away with this so easily!"

Richard's mind reeled as he sprinted down the steps. *Wherever Georgiana is, at least I know she is out of Lord Hugh's grasp* filled his senses while Lord Hugh's parting words echoed in his mind.

As he reached the bottom step, he saw Alex's hand waving at him from above the crowd. He made his way to where Alex and Rebecca stood next to an ornate fountain of a fish spurting water out of its mouth. Alex pointed towards the front doors.

Richard needed no other explanation. He knew on the other side of the doors he would find the woman he loved.

As he burst through the double doors, a cold icy blast of wintry air hitting him full in the face and chest. There, standing with her back to him, leaning on the balustrade, was Georgiana. The relief that flooded through his body made him want to laugh out loud. Instead, he crossed the short distance between them, pulled her away from the rail, spun her around, and enfolded her in his arms.

At first, she resisted when he tugged at her shoulders; but as soon as she saw who it was, she flung herself into his embrace.

There was no need for words. Richard could not find them even if he had wanted to. His only overwhelming desire was to hold her tightly and know that she was completely safe with him. He did not want to ever let her go.

It wasn't long before he realised that she was sobbing. He suspected he knew the reason, but now was not the place or the time to ask. He held her close and let her weep as he kissed the top of her head.

It was a few minutes before the tears abated. She sniffled into his waistcoat, clinging on to him for dear life. They remained thus for some time.

As the frigid night seeped into their bones, she looked up at him pleadingly with a tearstained face and asked, "Can we go home now?"

Richard nodded. "Of course," he replied, bent his head, and kissed her tenderly on the forehead.

Twenty-two

That night, Richard was awoken in the early hours. Hobbs tapped on the door, hissing his name.

Richard groggily rolled over in bed and kicked the blankets off. "Dear God, it's freezing!" The shock of the cold snapped him wide awake.

He stuffed his feet into his slippers, grabbed his dressing gown, pulled it tightly around him, and shuffled to his bedroom door.

"What is it, Hobbs?"

"I'm sorry to disturb you, Colonel Fitzwilliam, sir." Hobbs susurrated through the crack in the door. "But we've got a bit of the situation."

Richard opened the door wider and let the man in. He rubbed his hands together, shivering. "Is anyone awake to light me a fire? I can see my own breath."

"That is what I want to speak to you about, sir."

Richard looked the man up and down. Not only was the man dressed in pyjamas and dressing gown, but he had his greatcoat on and wore thick socks. "Right. Go on."

"The temperature, sir. It's plunged since we all retired for the night."

Richard nodded. That much was obvious.

"With my estimations, sir, we only have enough coal to last to the end of the day. The house is frozen." The man looked tired and worry-worn.

"Then procure some more tomorrow morning." Richard shrugged, wishing he could go back to bed.

"That's just it, Colonel Fitzwilliam, sir. The whole of London will be suffering in this cold snap. I've woken up the chambermaids. They'll light fires in the family bedrooms as soon as they are ready." Hobbs hesitated.

"And..."

"I wondered if I could have permission to venture out and purchase coal now."

Richard almost burst out laughing. "My dear man, if you believe you need to get more coal in, then do it. In the future, don't wake me and ask me. If it is this desperate, then just go. I trust you, Hobbs, to make the right decision.

Hobbs' expression of concern was immediately wiped away by relief. "Thank you, sir."

Richard turned back to his inviting bed. "Is there anything else?"

"Actually, sir, there is. The front and back doors..."

"What about them?" Richard frowned back at him.

"They're stuck fast. Nobody can get in or out."

"What?" he replied, rubbing the heel of his hand above the bridge of his nose, a sudden headache coming on.

"We've tried running tepid water over the locks, we've tried oiling them, and using brute force, but neither myself nor the footmen can budge them an inch. We wondered if you could give us a hand."

Richard shook his head, exhaling heavily. "All right. Give me a minute to get dressed and come down."

Hobbs bowed curtly. "Right you are, sir," he replied, exiting the room.

Richard huffed and strode to the window, pulling open the curtains. He could see nothing through the window. Jack Frost had done his most terrible work that night. The panes of glass were thick with ice on the inside. "My God," Richard breathed, his breath clouding before him. "How cold is it?"

Richard dressed in haste and arrived in the kitchens to see the two footmen and Hobbs doing their level best to pull the back door open. "Has anyone tried the window?" he asked.

The two footmen looked at each other wide-eyed, the answer plain to see.

"Right," Richard replied, rubbing his hands together rapidly. "Let's give it a try, shall we?"

The kitchen was warming up, as the range had been lit and hot water was heating on it. But even that and the physical exertion from trying to get the windows open did little to warm them.

The window pane cracked ominously as the two footmen stood on the cupboard before it and pushed with all their might to open the sash.

"Paying for a window to be replaced will be cheaper than having a locksmith come to fit a new lock if we must smash our way out of the back door," Richard encouraged them.

With a great gasp from the cook and housemaids, the window gave way. Alas, it opened little more than an inch. The footmen recoiled at the blast of freezing air that came in through the gap.

In a flash, Richard was up on the cupboard with the footmen. He shoved his hands through the freezing cold gap in the window and instructed the footmen to do the same. "Right, on the count of three...ready?"

"Ready," they chorused.

"One... Two... Three..."

Together they pushed with all their might and the window unwillingly slid upwards. The casement groaned and protested. Some of the wood snapped but, as they redoubled their efforts, the sash continued to open.

The three men sat back on their haunches, breathing deeply. The window had opened approximately one foot wide.

"Right," Richard said, jumping back down off the cupboard. "Which one of you thinks he can get through that gap?"

Alarmed, the two footmen gawped at him.

"Come on," Richard pushed. "Someone's got to get through that gap."

The two footmen continued to gape.

"Oh, for goodness sake!" Richard cried, stripping off down to his shirt and trousers. "I'll do it myself."

Richard hopped back onto the cupboard as the footmen climbed down. He braced himself. He knew it was going to be difficult, and once he got through the window, he would have to contend with the ice-covered ground beneath them.

He took a deep breath and pushed his head and shoulders through the gap. Richard let out a groan of pain. He overestimated the gap and underestimated his proportions. He had been certain a person could squeeze through. *What a shame we don't have a young lad in our employ*, he reflected.

As he wriggled his body, inching further through the window, he felt the cupboard shift behind him. The footmen climbed back up and were doing their best to force the window open another inch or two, giving Richard more room.

As he heaved his body forward, his chest became constricted, and it was difficult to breathe. However, he had gone so far that there was no turning back. Either way, he knew it was going to hurt.

With a great yell, Richard placed his hands against the frozen brickwork, and shoved hard, using his feet for leverage. He was now out of the window up to his waist. His chest was free but the skin over one of his ribs burnt with pain. He took deep gulps of air, which didn't make him feel any better. The air was icy and felt like razor blades in his lungs.

"Give my feet a push," he called out, the blood rushing to his head.

The footmen dismounted the cabinet and did as they were asked.

Together with the footmen shoving his feet and Richard thrusting against the bricks, he broke free and fell tumbling to the hard-frozen ground.

For a moment or two, Richard stared up at the black starry sky, the wind knocked out of him. He closed his eyes in pain.

Slowly he regained the ability to breathe in and out, the cold seeping deep into his bones and reviving him. Richard clambered awkwardly to his feet, knocking the dirt off his hands and clothes. He looked down at his shirt. His flesh, bloodied and grazed, stared back at him through a gaping hole. However, that was the least of his worries. He checked the windowpane and was pleased to discover the damage was limited.

Richard then turned his attention to the back door. "Toss me my gloves," Richard called back through the window. The gloves flew out of the window and he caught them. He was grateful to shove his icy fingers into the fur-lined leather.

"All right," he called. "Again on three. Ready?"

He heard the footmen and Hobbs call back that they were.

Richard gripped the door handle and placed one foot against the brickwork. "One... Two... Three..."

Between them they pushed and pulled as the door creaked, groaned, and stubbornly remained stuck. Frantically, the men continued their persuasion until, suddenly, it burst open, knocking Richard onto his back. Again he was winded.

He gasped for air as Hobbs and the footmen rushed out to his aid. They carried him inside and sat him on a chair before the range. Slowly, he began to breathe normally again. He rubbed at his ribs which felt bruised from the abuse.

"Well," Richard panted. "At least the door is open."

He watched as Hobbs returned outside and examined something on the wall before re-entering the kitchen and pulling the door closed a little.

"What's the temperature?" Richard asked. "What does the thermometer say?"

"You won't believe this, sir." Hobbs blew on his hands. "The thermometer is completely frozen over. The mercury is right down at the bottom. God only knows how cold it is out there."

Richard whistled. "Make sure everyone stays inside today, if they can. Let's keep this house as warm as possible."

"Yes, sir."

Once he was recovered and had drunk a cup of tea, Richard returned to bed while Hobbs ventured out and procured more coal.

As Richard drifted back off to sleep, he was glad neither his mother nor cousin had been awakened by the shenanigans below stairs. His mother would have been mortified to see him scrambling through the window. He smiled at the idea of her catching him.

At least the house is warming up now and the ladies won't freeze, he thought gratefully as he drifted off.

Twenty-three

When Georgiana awoke, she lay staring up at the ceiling. It took a moment to realise she could hear the sound of crackling fire. She hoisted herself up onto her elbows and frowned. Usually the fire was only lit when it was time for her to wake up.

She slipped out of bed and tiptoed to the window. "Oh!" she exclaimed, surveying the iced-up window. She hurried back to the bed, put her feet into her slippers, and wrapped herself in a blanket. "At least now I know why there is a fire." She rang the bell for Meg and sat before the fire brushing her hair. She tried to think back to a time when the windows were so iced up on the inside at Pemberley. She could not recall ever seeing them so. It was not uncommon for a little ice on the inside during winter, but not for every single window pane to be entirely iced over.

Half an hour later, dressed in a heavy brocade dress with long sleeves and a shawl around her shoulders, Georgiana scuttled down the stairs to the breakfast room. She found Aunt Henrietta and Richard there already.

"Oh, Georgiana, my dear! Are you warm enough?" Aunt Henrietta cried as soon as she set eyes on her niece.

"I am now I'm dressed, Aunt." Georgiana replied, joining them at the table.

"Can you believe what a frightful frost we've had this morning?" her aunt asked, passing her the rack of hot toast.

"I don't believe I've ever seen anything like it." Georgiana helped herself.

"It is possible that it is as cold as it was last year." Richard joined in the conversation. "All of society was abuzz with talk about the Frost Fair on the Thames last year."

Georgiana stopped buttering her toast and raised her eyes. "Frost Fair?"

"Oh, yes! They had foxhunting, bull-baiting, football matches, and even ninepin bowling on the ice. Alex was here last year, and he said they even roasted an ox on the ice. It was so thick that the ox was roasting for twenty-four hours. Can you believe it?" he wriggled his eyebrows.

Georgiana shook her head, completely agog. "That is incredible!"

"It is a little foolhardy, if you ask me. Imagine having a fire on ice!" Aunt Henrietta shuddered. "It does not bear thinking about what would have happened had they melted a hole right through to the Thames." Her shoulders shook again.

Georgiana watched Richard smile indulgently at his mother.

"It is of very little consequence now, Mama, for it is in the past and what is done is done.

"Well," Aunt Henrietta pursed her lips together, "I still maintain it was a very foolish thing to do."

Richard chuckled. "There is no doubt about it, Mama, but a great deal of fun was had by all, I daresay." He winked at Georgiana.

Aunt Henrietta clicked her tongue against the roof of her mouth disapprovingly.

Richard changed the subject and discussed the procurement of food and coal.

Georgiana concentrated on her breakfast. She was glad no one had asked her what happened the night before. Not a single syllable was uttered on the subject. She was grateful to have a family that loved her in such a way that they did not need her to justify herself. As she crunched a piece of toast between her teeth, she hoped the night before would be the last time she would ever have to hear from or see Lord Hugh. She trusted she had made herself perfectly clear.

As soon as breakfast was over, the bell to the front door rang. Georgiana's heart jumped into her mouth. Her heart pounded in her chest. For a short rebellious moment, she wanted to cry out, "Don't answer it! Let's pretend we're not here."

She pushed the impulse away and hesitated in the breakfast room instead of following her aunt and cousin into the entrance hall.

A familiar voice reached her ears, and she tittered with relief. She turned around and burst through the breakfast room door, greeting their guests with a wide smile. “Alex! Rebecca! Whatever made you venture out in this inhospitable weather?” she asked.

Richard stifled a snigger. “That is precisely what I just asked them.”

Aunt Henrietta pulled her shawl closer about her shoulders. “Come in, the pair of you! You’re letting all the heat out.” She turned about and disappeared into the drawing room. The rest followed her.

Seating themselves around the blazing fire, Alex, a silly grin planted on his face, addressed Georgiana. “We have come with some rather interesting news, Miss Darcy.”

Georgiana’s face lit up, and she shuffled to the edge of her seat. “Oh, aye?”

“Aye, indeed.” Rebecca giggled.

“No one knows the exact temperature outside, as yet,” Alex explained, “but many folks are saying that it is a least minus four degrees Fahrenheit.”

Georgiana gasped and covered her mouth with her hands.

“Dear Lord!” Aunt Henrietta exclaimed and shuffled a little closer to the fire as though it were minus four in the drawing room.

“Apparently, though, it isn’t quite as cold as last year. The Thames hasn’t frozen over completely,” Alex continued.

The corners of Georgiana's mouth turned down. She felt a little disappointed by Alex's revelation. The thought of experiencing the things Richard had mentioned filled her with anticipation.

"However," Alex drew out the word, his eyes dancing with mischief, "a lot of the Thames *has* frozen up."

Georgiana clapped her hands together, her excitement rekindled.

"Rebecca and I were wondering if you, Miss Darcy, and you, of course, Richard," he pulled a face at his friend, "would like to join us for a spot of ice-skating on the River Thames."

"Oh, my goodness!" Georgiana squealed with delight.

Richard burst out laughing. "I think that is a yes."

"So do I," Alex agreed, laughing too.

Rebecca shot across the room, sat next to Georgiana, and took hold of her hands. "We shall be such a merry bunch. We shall have hot chestnuts, for Alex says there will be many food vendors pitching their pop-up stalls on the ice."

Georgiana could scarcely believe it. The fishing lakes at Pemberley would often freeze over at Christmas and during the winter. When she was a child, her brother would regularly take her ice-skating, as long as the ice held his weight first, but the idea that the river at the heart of the city was frozen over, if only for a day or two, and that all the inhabitants of London could possibly be frolicking there left her awestruck.

"Just be sure that whatever you eat is fresh and well cooked," Aunt Henrietta said, waggling a warning finger in Georgiana's direction.

She deflated a little. "Yes, Aunt."

"Mama," Richard rushed to her defence, "I assure you that Georgiana will be well taken care of. I would not let anything happen to her."

He smiled at her, and her stomach backflipped.

"When shall we depart?" Rebecca asked.

"The sooner these two can make themselves ready, the better," Alex replied, grinning broadly.

Georgiana could not have exited the room any faster.

* * *

Fresh hot bricks were prepared for Alex's carriage, and amid cautionary warnings from Aunt Henrietta, the four of them set out for the river.

At first, Georgiana felt overly dressed; that was until she stepped out into the frigid air. She realised then that all the layers Aunt Henrietta had insisted upon had their value. She protested at wearing sheepskin, fur-lined mittens, and taking a muff, but understood now that her aunt was far wiser.

So far during her stay, Georgiana had not ventured so close to the river. She pressed herself close to the window. She did not want to miss a thing.

"There is, of course, one good thing to be said for the Thames freezing over," Alex chortled, "one cannot smell the sewage in the river so much."

Startled, Georgiana twisted around in her seat. "The sewage goes into the river?"

"As it does everywhere," Alex replied.

"But in a city this size..." Georgiana's mouth fell open, and she stared back out the window.

"My cousin does have a point," Richard added. "I believe there are some cities in Europe now that have reached such a size they are installing plumbing."

"Like the Romans had?" Rebecca asked.

"I believe modern plumbing is based upon that idea, yes."

"Then they ought to do that here too," Georgiana breathed against the window, fogging it up.

"Indeed, they jolly well should!" Alex slapped his knee. "You remember Horace?" he asked Richard.

Georgiana sat back properly, interested in the conversation.

"Horace Albright? Pimple-faced chap?" Richard squinted in recollection.

"Aye," Alex acknowledged, "that's the fellow. Well, he's a doctor here in London now, and the things he tells me would shock even the hardiest of soldiers."

Richard raised a shoulder in his thick grey woollen coat. "I don't know. I've seen some terrible things in my time."

"He says that whenever we have an insufferably hot and humid summer—"

"Which is most years," Richard interrupted.

"Apart from the last," Alex snorted. "Well, Horace says that during those summers, here in London they have the most horrific outbreaks of cholera."

Georgiana's hand shot to her mouth.

"Oh, my goodness!" Rebecca balked.

Richard groaned. "I have seen my fair share of cholera cases, I can tell you. Dear God! I would not wish that upon my worst enemy."

"Then something ought to be done!" Georgiana blurted out.

"Indeed," Alex agreed with her. "But by whom?"

Georgiana frowned. She had no idea.

"Only the ruling classes can petition such changes," Richard explained. "How many of them are really interested in whether the poorer working-class folk catch cholera or not?"

"That is heartless!" she cried.

"Yes, it is," Richard replied, laying his hand over hers and causing her heart to flutter and stilling her tongue.

Alex sighed and laid his head back. "Aye, progress and change are slow, but there is one thing for certain...you cannot stop them."

Georgiana could not explain why, but his words gave her some comfort. Growing up, Georgiana had always been impressed upon by her brother and her parents to take care of those who were less fortunate than she. It grieved her deeply that there were those living within the confines of London who suffered. She decided that, when she got back to Pemberley, she would ask her brother about the sewage upon the estate. No woman could vote, but women could change things, she knew. She might help and make a start with Pemberley. As her brother always told her, a rockfall always began with a small pebble.

Twenty-four

Richard was astounded by how many people crammed onto the ice that morning. They hired skates and tentatively stepped out onto the frozen river. It had been many years since Richard had the opportunity to ice-skate and his feet were unsteady beneath him. Luckily for him, Georgiana came to his rescue by taking hold of his hand. Despite them both wearing thick gloves, Richard imagined he could feel the warmth of her skin upon his.

"Look!" Georgiana pointed as they skated past a metal brazier burning fiercely hot on the ice. "The ice must be thick indeed."

The notion of hot metal and fire started Richard's knees trembling. One of his skates slipped beneath him.

Georgiana tugged his arm closer to her, steadying him. "Careful!"

Richard was glad she was there. If she had not been, most likely he would have landed on his behind most inelegantly. He called out to Alex, "How thick do you think the ice is?"

"Who cares?" he cried back, skating off ahead with Rebecca.

It took a few more minutes for Richard to find his balance and remember how to skate. For him, the key was not to think about the depth of the ice beneath him, nor the frigid river beneath that.

After a while of skating in silence, Richard looked down and watched Georgiana confidently and effortlessly gliding along beside him as though she were born on the ice.

"Georgiana," he spoke, his voice catching as she upturned her head to look back at him, squinting in the sunlight.

"What is it?" she asked.

"Georgiana, forgive me if I am being impertinent and overstepping the line, but..." Richard hesitated, unsure if he should plough on.

"Go on," Georgiana prompted. "You can ask me anything."

Richard swallowed as they swerved to avoid another couple skating towards them. "What happened with Lord Hugh last night?"

He watched her face fall and regretted asking. "I'm sorry. I shouldn't pry."

Georgiana shook her head and gave his hand an encouraging squeeze. "It is quite all right, Richard. It's just..." she hesitated. "It's just that I do not like even thinking about Lord Hugh."

At her confession, Richard wanted to pry. He wanted to know what happened between them. He desperately yearned to know if there was anything he could do to help the young lady beside him who had captured his heart. Instead, he skated on in silence hoping Georgiana would find the words to express herself.

"I'm afraid, dearest cousin, I have been frightfully foolish yet again." Georgiana did not look in his direction but remained staring at a fixed point ahead of them.

Richard, however, kept his eyes firmly on her.

"I promised myself that I would never be so foolish as to allow a man to persuade me that I was in love." She huffed, her breath trailing out in a cloud behind them as they traversed their way around a group of children learning to skate. "And yet all it took was a little flattery, a handsome face, and some attention on Lord Hugh's part to make me lose my head again." She momentarily glanced back at him. "Oh, do not get me wrong. I was never in love with Lord Hugh...well, not as I perceive true love to be anyway. But to my eternal shame, it did not take very much persuasion on his part to have me fancying myself enamoured."

They skated on in silence for a little while. Richard was unable to find the words to console his cousin. They both smiled and waved cheerily as Alex and Rebecca lapped them.

"After a short visit, Lord Hugh believed there was an understanding between us." Georgiana shook her head. "I don't know…" She huffed. "I may have said something foolish enough to give him hope. But if I did, I do not remember what it was."

They turned around and skated back in the direction they had come.

"I know that your mother would have simply called it a harmless flirtation. Nevertheless, Lord Hugh certainly took it far more seriously." She sniffed and rubbed her nose with the back of her mitten. "If I'm entirely honest with you, Richard," she glanced at him, this time holding his gaze for a second or two before continuing, "I did not spare Lord Hugh a single thought between visits."

Her words filled him with hope. He held his breath.

"It was then that I realised anything that had passed between myself and Lord Hugh was just that—a harmless flirtation and nothing more."

Richard's heart hammered, and he slowly released the breath he was holding.

"From then on, I did my level best to distance myself from him. My intention was to let him know as gently as possible that there was nothing serious between us and that he ought not raise his hopes on that account. Unfortunately, I underestimated his zeal."

Again, she fell silent, and Richard was unwilling to break the spell.

"I do not know if I am being childish, but there's just something about Lord Hugh that I do not trust. I cannot quite put my finger on it," she muttered.

Richard toyed with the idea of telling her all about Margaret Ainsworth and the illegitimate child she bore Lord Hugh but thought better of it. They were in a public place after all, and such a tale was more than likely to upset Georgiana rather than reassure her. The retelling could wait for another time.

They skated on and caught up with Alex and Rebecca, who waited for them close by a food stall.

"Anyone fancy roasted chestnuts?" Alex called out cheerily.

Together, the four of them shared a bag of chestnuts while sitting on the wall at the edge of the river.

Richard replayed Georgiana's confession in his mind. He wanted nothing more than to take her in his arms and to tell her he would never let anyone hurt her. But now was not the time. The story was not ended. She had mentioned nothing of last night's goings-on or of what happened in the dining room.

Alex shot off, leaving Richard with the two ladies wondering where he disappeared to. When he returned, he was carrying four tiny cups of hot mulled wine.

"Oh, my goodness! That does taste good," Rebecca cooed as she sipped.

"Yes," Georgiana tittered. "Now it feels like Christmas."

* * *

It was agreed that they would take another turn or two on the ice and then head back to Pembroke Square to warm themselves through. Georgiana had to admit that she could no longer feel her toes, and the promise of going home for hot chocolate and one of Cook's excellent mince pies was irresistibly tempting.

There was something reassuring and quite natural about holding Richard's hand while they skated along. It filled her with a warmth and belonging that she wished would reach down and warm up her feet. After they'd skated for a while in silence, Georgiana realised that Richard was waiting patiently for her to continue telling him about the night before. The last thing she wanted was for Richard to think ill of her, so she chose her words carefully.

"Do you remember last night when you and Alex went in search of George?" she asked.

"I do."

"That was when Lord Hugh sought me out to dance."

"Oh. I thought as much."

Georgiana watched Richard's face fall. "Do not blame yourself, Richard. I doubt very much you could have prevented it. And besides, I knew I had to tell him something.

The foolish man was under the impression that we were both head over heels in love with each other."

"And you are not?"

"No, Richard! I told you I was not in love with him." For an instant she thought she saw relief pass across his face but was unsure. "I have never been in love with him, and I can promise you wholeheartedly that I will never be in love with Lord Hugh DeVere."

She watched Richard's mouth curl into smile. This time she was far more certain of the relief she saw in his face.

"He started declaring very loudly that I had jilted him." Georgiana shook her head. "He was making a scene! I was mortified." She squinted up at Richard. "You don't believe him a simpleton, do you?"

Richard laughed bitterly and shook his head. "No, my dear Georgiana, I do not believe him a simpleton. Believe me," he held her hand tighter, "there are a great number of things that I could accuse Lord Hugh DeVere of being, but a simpleton is most certainly not one of them.

Once again, the inkling that Richard knew far more about Lord Hugh than he was letting on raised its head.

"What do you mean?" she asked.

Richard glanced furtively around them. "Not here and not now." They stopped skating and faced each other. "But believe me, Georgiana, I will tell you everything that I know."

Twenty-five

By the time the four of them drove back to Pembroke Square, it was snowing heavily.

As they pulled up in front of the house, Richard turned to Alex. "I think it would be best if you took Miss Hawkins directly home." He peered out at the sky. "This does not look like it's going to abate any time soon."

Alex reflected and agreed with his friend. "You're right. Well," he beamed at Georgiana, "it has been an absolute pleasure yet again to spend time with you, Miss Darcy. Let us hope the snow stops soon and we can repeat the pleasure, eh?"

Georgiana thought she had never been so happy in her whole life to make new acquaintance other than that of her sister-in-law, Elizabeth. She was growing increasingly fond of Rebecca and Alex. "I hope so too."

"Hurry into the house!" Rebecca bade.

Richard descended, turned back, and offered Georgiana his hand. She was grateful for his assistance. The snow was so heavy, it was falling on the tips of her eyelashes, and she could scarcely see the step to climb down. As she placed her winter boot upon the snow-covered tread, her foot slipped and she tumbled forward.

Richard's reflexes were lightning fast. One second Georgiana had the sensation of falling headlong forward, and the next she was being scooped up by Richard's strong arms and being held tight to his body. Her heart pounded in her ears, not just from the shock of slipping over, but from the intimacy. All too soon, he had her on terra firma, her heart pining for a repeat of the embrace.

"Are you all right?" Alex called from inside the carriage.

With her cheeks ablaze, Georgiana responded, "Quite all right, thank you." She was glad her blush could be attributed to embarrassment. Only Georgiana knew the real reason.

"We had best get inside before she takes another tumble," Richard chuckled.

Georgiana caught the expression on Richard's face. If she were not mistaken, his eyes reflected the same longing she felt. She stood motionless peering up at him through the falling snow.

"Cheerio, then!" Alex cried and disappeared back inside carriage.

Georgiana was acutely aware of Richard's bodily presence as they mounted the steps. Before they reached the front door, it swung open, revealing the butler.

"Colonel Fitzwilliam, sir. Miss Darcy. Welcome home." Hobbs held the door open wide, and Richard and Georgiana hurried inside. "I am ever so glad you are back," the butler continued, "for the mistress is in a right state."

"Is she all right?" Georgiana panted.

Hobbs reassured her that Aunt Henrietta was quite all right apart from being out of sorts and upset.

"The mistress received a visitor, sir."

Having taken off her outdoor things, Georgiana turned to Richard for guidance.

"We'd better go and see her," he said, striding past her and heading into the drawing room.

Aunt Henrietta was in her favourite chair beside the fireplace. She stared into the flames and did not look up when they entered. However, she made sniffling noises and Georgiana guessed she was crying.

"Mama," Richard said as he knelt down beside her, "whatever is the matter?"

"Oh, my dear boy! Whatever shall we do?" she sobbed.

Georgiana dug her hand into her pocket and retrieved her handkerchief. She handed it to her aunt, taking away her damp one and leaving it on a nearby table.

"Mrs Fotheringhay came to pay me a visit this morning." She sniffed and blew her nose.

Richard and Georgiana glanced at each other, puzzled.

"And?" Richard asked.

"She said she came to share some gossip with me." Aunt Henrietta took a deep juddering breath. "Mrs Fotheringhay told me that she heard among the ladies of the *ton* about Georgiana and Lord Hugh DeVere."

Richard groaned and hung his head.

Georgiana was aghast. She stepped backwards until she fell onto the settee behind her.

Aunt Henrietta's eyes welled with tears which spilled over and ran down her cheeks. "She then had the audacity to congratulate me on the forthcoming nuptials of my niece to Lord Hugh DeVere."

Georgiana swallowed, her stomach sank down into her boots.

"Mama, I can assure you that Georgiana has never been engaged to marry Lord Hugh." Richard said vehemently, taking hold of one of his mother's hands. "He has invented the whole thing."

Aunt Henrietta looked up. Her eyes locked with Georgiana's and the latter could see the pain within. "I should never have encouraged him, Georgiana."

"These rumours will die down in time when no wedding is forthcoming," Richard mumbled. "It is something we must endure, I'm afraid."

"But don't you see?" Aunt Henrietta wept. "He is telling everyone in town that he and Georgiana are to be wed."

"So you said. It is a lie, is it not, Georgiana?" Richard spoke with ardour. His eyes willed her to speak out.

"Of course, it is!" Georgiana fairly screeched.

"That is not what worries me." Aunt Henrietta wiped at her face with the handkerchief. "If Lord Hugh persists in his assertion of their engagement while Georgina simply denies it, he may claim that Georgiana has jilted him! She will have her reputation sullied. Which gentlemen would want to court a woman if he fears she might jilt him too?"

"Damn him!" Richard blasted, rose to his feet and stomped about the room in thought.

Georgiana could see precisely what her aunt was getting at. Lord Hugh was ensuring that, if he could not have Georgiana, then he would make sure that it was near impossible for her to find any other man. Her stomach knotted. Tears filled her own eyes. "I wish had never come to London. I wish I had never laid eyes on Lord Hugh DeVere." She sniffed back the tears and angrily wiped her face with the back of her hand.

"Whatever shall we do?" Aunt Henrietta asked. "We must think of something to counter this slander and safeguard Georgiana's reputation."

"Don't you worry, Mama." Richard stopped pacing and stared out of the window, his voice a threatening growl. "I will make certain of it one way or another."

* * *

The atmosphere in the house was heavy and the conversation stilted from then on. Georgiana felt miserable and wretched, Aunt Henrietta repeatedly declared that she blamed herself, and Richard did his best to steer the discussion away every time the subject came up.

The snow continued to fall heavily well into the afternoon. A welcome respite arrived in the form of hot buttered crumpets and tea at three o'clock in the afternoon.

The mood lifted with the advent of something to eat and drink. Georgiana took Richard's lead and told her aunt all about skating on the River Thames.

By the time tea was over, Aunt Henrietta was complaining of a thunderous headache. "It is all the weeping, no doubt," she said wearily, rising from the armchair and heading towards the door. "I think I shall take my dinner in my room tonight." Standing in the doorway, she turned and addressed Georgiana. "I am frightfully sorry, my dear. I ought never to have encouraged that man, and I most certainly should never have teased you. Forgive me."

In an instant, Georgiana was out of her seat and running across the room into her aunt's arms. "Aunt Henrietta, there is nothing to forgive." She squeezed her tight. "The man was determined to make mischief. He knew what he wanted and set out to get it. When he couldn't, he decided to destroy it."

Aunt Henrietta's bottom lip trembled.

"I shall bear it, Aunt." She pulled back and smiled. "And if anyone should utter a single syllable on the subject within my hearing, I shall have no compunction in telling them precisely what a horrid, odious man Lord Hugh is."

Aunt Henrietta chuckled. "That's the spirit, my girl. We'll get through this, and any man worth his salt will see you for the treasure you are." She kissed Georgiana on the forehead and left them alone.

Georgiana closed the door behind her aunt and returned to the settee, wishing there were some more crumpets left. She glanced over Richard. "Would you think me gluttonous if I called for some more crumpets?"

Richard chortled and pulled a face. "No, because I might beat you to it!"

Georgiana rang the bell and asked Hobbs if they might have some more crumpets. He returned in no time at all bearing a tray with another pot of tea and yet another plate of hot buttered crumpets.

"Mmm...this is just what I need." Georgiana sighed as she picked up two and put them on a cake plate.

Richard followed suit and sat down opposite her. They ate on in silence for a few minutes before Richard asked, "Do you want me to tell you what I know about Lord Hugh now?"

Georgiana almost dropped the crumpet in her hand. "Yes."

Twenty-six

Richard observed his cousin all afternoon. Whilst she appeared hurt and upset by what Lord Hugh was attempting to do to her reputation, she handled it well. Once he heard her words to his mother, he realised he had no cause for concern whatsoever. They both came from strong, hardy stock, and he was proud to discover that she too possessed the family's fighting spirit.

He decided that now was better than later to tell her all he knew about Lord Hugh and his reputation for philandry. He just had to think how to phrase it without alarming her.

Richard rose and crossed to the window. He peeked out at the sky. The sun was now setting behind the houses in front, and Richard was relieved to see the snow had stopped falling.

"Georgiana!" Richard cried out, as his eyes fell on the scene before him on the road.

In an instant, Georgiana was on her feet and by his side. "Whatever is it?"

"Look!" Richard pointed.

The snow that afternoon had fallen thick and fast, settling a hefty layer covering everything and silencing the world. From around the corner came a carriage on sleigh tracks, its occupants giggling with excitement.

"Oh, my word!" she exclaimed.

Richard looked down as Georgiana's face lit up like a candelabra. They watched the carriage's progression down the street and, to the delight of both, another one followed as the first passed out of view. This one's occupants were mainly children whose excitement bubbled over.

"What would you say if I had sleigh tracks put on our carriage?" Richard asked as his cousin's upturned face answered him immediately. "We could take a ride together."

"Oh, yes! That would be delightful!" Georgiana turned back to the wintry scene outside the window, almost pressing her nose against the ice-cold pane.

"I'm quite certain that Mama would have no objections if we converted the old phaeton." In a flash, Richard left the room in search of Hobbs.

Richard didn't miss the look of exasperation on Hobbs' face. He pushed it to one side. He realised the man was getting on a little bit in years, but it wasn't as though he would personally have to put the sleigh tracks onto the carriage. He wondered briefly, as he headed back into the drawing room, if they hadn't been overly lenient with him.

"Right." Richard clapped his hands and rubbed them together. "That's that all sorted. Now, Georgiana," he crossed to her and laid his hands upon her shoulders, "let's get ourselves prepared to brace the chill winter evening, shall we?"

Richard led the way upstairs to the bedrooms. He did not know which one of them was the most excited, himself or Georgiana. As he bounded into his room, changed into a pair of thick socks, and retrieved his greatcoat, scarf, and mittens, Richard saw it all as a stroke of luck. It would be far easier to explain about Margaret's baby and Lord Hugh's reputation while they were driving along and enjoying such a beautiful wintry scene.

Richard arrived back down in the entrance hall before Georgiana and had the pleasure of watching her descend the stairs. She was elegantly dressed in a long deep green woollen pelisse with matching fur-trimmed scarf, gloves, and bonnet. Richard's heart stopped. *She is perfection itself,* he thought. He blinked rapidly to clear his mind. "You look wonderfully warm."

"It is my intention to remain so," she giggled, lifting up the blanket in her hand. "Whilst it is fun and exciting to take a sleigh ride in the snow," she quipped, checking her scarf was tight enough around her neck, "the last thing either of us wants is to come back with a ghastly cold and with our extremities like blocks of ice."

"You are quite right," Richard chuckled along with her. "It would dampen the spirits somewhat if we were to freeze to death."

Hobbs appeared, informing them the phaeton was ready, and together they rushed headlong out of the house and climbed into the waiting carriage.

Richard dismissed the driver, took hold of the reins himself, and they set off, sliding along the snow.

For a while neither of them spoke a word, simply enjoyed the night and each other's company. Richard, however, knew he had made a promise to tell his cousin everything he knew about Lord Hugh. He had no idea how his cousin would take it nor how she would likely be affected by the sad tale of Margaret Ainsworth. Mentally he checked his pocket for a handkerchief. He never felt fully dressed unless he had one seconded somewhere about his person.

"I believe now is as good a time as any for me to tell you about Lord Hugh." Richard moved so he could see his cousin's face.

The smile she wore slipped. "Oh. Very well then."

"I do not wish to ruin this beautiful evening, but this night might take away some of the ugliness of what I'm about to tell you."

He watched Georgiana settle into the corner of the phaeton, ready to listen to all he had to say; then he turned his attention back to the road before taking a deep breath and beginning with rumours that reached his ears when they first arrived in London.

Throughout the telling, Georgiana remained stock still. She did not utter a word or even move a muscle until he was done.

"And this is the man who wishes to marry me," she breathed, her voice heavy with sadness.

"I'm afraid so." Richard glanced back at her. He could not read her expression.

As the silence dragged on, Richard wondered whether he should turn the phaeton about and head home when Georgiana finally spoke up.

"And what is to be done?"

"About Lord Hugh?" Richard sputtered. "I had not thought to do anything about him. Other than to tell you, that is. I do not wish to be responsible for ruining the man's reputation."

"It seems he is doing very well at ruining his own reputation, wouldn't you say?"

Richard had to admit she was correct.

"No, what I meant was, what is to be done about Margaret Ainsworth and the child?"

"What do you mean?" Richard's eyes traversed her face in an attempt to read her mind.

Georgiana sat upright and shuffled a little closer to him. An involuntary smile graced his lips at her proximity. "What I wish to know is who is taking care of Margaret and the child? You said her father was without work now."

"He has a small income."

Georgiana snorted. "The sum you told me is hardly sufficient for Mr Ainsworth, two daughters, a grandson, and servants. What is Lord Hugh to do? Does the Duke of

Somerset know about his grandchild?" She slipped her arm into Richard's, snuggling up to him.

"I'm afraid to say the Duke of Somerset does know about little Walter. And, no, neither is doing anything about it."

"So she is entirely friendless," Georgiana's voice faltered, and she laid her head against Richard's arm.

She feels it deeply. Richard wanted nothing more than to stop the carriage and hold her. Yet he did not. He feared she did not feel for him as he felt for her. *Could she ever love me?*

"What kind of trade does her father have?" Georgiana asked him.

"He used to work as a bookkeeper for a bank here in London," he informed her.

She frowned in thought. "Can a position not be found for him in Bournemouth?"

"I do not have any contacts in Bournemouth, I'm afraid," Richard confessed. "Or else I would help the man."

"What about private work?" Georgiana sat bolt upright, turned and faced him. "Will Alex not need a bookkeeper or accountant when he is married?"

Richard was overwhelmed by her questions but touched by her compassion and desperation to help the family. "I cannot rightly say. I have no idea how Alex's finances are arranged. At present, I believe his father handles his allowance."

"And when he is married and has a household of his own," Georgiana splayed out a gloved hand, opening her eyes wide, "he will need to take on someone to make sure he does not exceed his income, will he not?"

Richard chuckled. "Most gentlemen do that themselves."

He watched Georgiana frown and pursed her lips at him. "Surely it would be more prudent to have a professional look at the account's ledgers, would it not?"

Richard laughed harder. Finally, he understood her train of thought. "Yes," he grinned, "I believe it would be most prudent to have one's own bookkeeper."

Seemingly content that Richard now understood her, Georgiana laid her head back upon his shoulder. "And it would be even more prudent to keep that bookkeeper on a retainer throughout the year, do you not think?"

Richard could not prevent himself from chuckling at her audacity. "You are quite right, dearest Georgiana." The laughter stopped, and his voice deepened. "It is much better to allow the man to provide for his own family rather than giving him charity."

"He is quite likely too proud to accept charity."

"Again, you are right." He rotated his head as she lifted hers, and he gazed lovingly into her eyes. "Your compassion astounds me."

Richard could see she held her breath.

Her voice was thick with emotion when she spoke. "Surely any decent human being would feel the same."

"I fear that these days, they are few and far between."

A cry ahead forced Richard's eyes back on the road only to discover the carriage had drifted to the right and into the path of an oncoming carriage. He was embarrassed he lost control, but even more, he lamented losing the moment between them.

As Georgiana settled back, nestling against him, Richard turned the carriage towards the river, wondering what was going on there that evening.

* * *

Georgiana saw the signpost and knew Richard steered them towards the river. She was curious to discover what was happening on the frozen river. Long before they even reach the riverbanks, they heard strains of music on the air, singing, and the unmistakable sound of merrymaking.

Georgiana smiled at Richard as he gazed down at her. "It sounds to me as though London is thoroughly enjoying this particularly cold snap in the weather." He grinned.

"Indeed, I believe she is." Georgiana's stomach fluttered with excitement.

"The least we could do is stop for a cup of mulled wine, should they have any," Richard shrugged.

Georgiana giggled. "It would not be in keeping with the festive spirit were we to pass up such an opportunity."

"Indeed, you are right." Richard sniggered and spurred the horses on. "I believe it is our civic duty to participate."

Georgiana gripped his arm tighter, buried her face in his sleeve, and laughed. "Besides, we cannot very well report back to your mother if we have absolutely no experience of the festivities whatsoever."

Richard threw back his head and laughed in a way that made Georgiana's heart soar. "Do you know, I believe you're right!"

The pair of them, infected by the contagious Christmas spirit, laughed and joked as they parked the carriage amongst the others beside the river bank. Georgiana wished the night would never end. She did not believe she had ever felt so contented, and she never wanted to leave Richard's side.

Richard helped her to dismount, and together they made their way onto the ice.

"Look! Over there!" Richard pointed. He bent his head down so close to her face that she could feel his breath on her skin. "Let's get some mulled wine to warm us through."

Georgiana merely nodded, unsure whether she could find enough voice to answer.

The mulled wine certainly did its trick. The hot spicy beverage burned its way down Georgiana's throat and into her stomach, warming her much faster than she expected.

She spied a Punch and Judy puppet show, and they made their way towards it. "I haven't seen one of these since I was a little girl," she cried out to be heard.

"I remember how well you loved it whenever the travelling fair came to Lambton."

They stood with the other revellers, men, women, and children alike, watching the performance put on by the puppeteer.

Their enjoyment was cut short by the screeching sound of a voice Georgiana hoped she would not have to endure again.

"Cooey! Miss Darcy!" the disembodied voice cried out.

Richard turned around and complained in Georgiana's ear. "Dear God in heaven! Spare us."

"Miss Darcy! Oh, it is you!" Lady Francesca reached them. "My brother said it couldn't possibly have been you, for he believes you at home, but it is! Imagine my surprise."

Georgiana's eyes darted around the sea of people at the mention of Lady Francesca's brother. She was gratified when Richard took a protective step closer to her. She clung on tighter to his arm, her heart pounding in her chest at the thought that any moment now Lord Hugh would appear from out of the crowd.

"What unseasonable weather we're having!" Lady Francesca pouted.

Georgiana hid a smile as Richard scowled at the Duke's daughter. "What do you mean unseasonable? It is winter, and it is freezing. In my experience, the two go hand-in-hand."

"How droll you are, Colonel Fitzwilliam!" She chortled falsely and flapped a mitten in his direction. "I am aware that it is winter, and it is perfectly normal to have freezing temperatures, but even you must admit these are unusual."

Richard bowed. "You are right."

Georgiana felt him tense beside her. She did her level best to think of a reason to depart so soon after their arrival.

Lady Francesca gushed with happiness. "I am so excited for you, my dear Georgiana!"

"Oh?"

Lady Francesca tapped her playfully on the arm. "Yes, silly! My brother told me this morning." She grinned at them expectantly.

Both Georgiana and Richard were nonplussed. Georgiana blinked at her.

"Oh! How you can contain your excitement is beyond me," she squealed.

Cautiously Georgiana replied, "Excitement? Excitement about what?"

"About your engagement to my brother!" Lady Francesca clapped her gloved hands together. "I can tell you most sincerely that Hugh has not talked of anything else all day."

Georgiana felt her knees go weak and buckle underneath her. "I..."

Richard put his arm around her waist and held her steady.

"Hugh says he will travel to Somerset to see father and ask his permission tomorrow morning." She beamed at them. "Just think, Georgiana! By the summer you and I will be sisters."

Georgiana trembled with fear until she realised that Richard, standing so close to her, was also trembling. She glanced up into his face and saw fury there.

"I beg your pardon, Lady Francesca, but I believe you are mistaken." Richard's voice contained no hint of friendliness.

"Indeed, I am not." Lady Francesca stuck out her chin. "My brother informed me this morning that he proposed to Miss Darcy last night at the charity ball." She leant a little closer to Richard, unafraid of his stature or the edge to his voice. "My brother says that Miss Darcy accepted his proposal and that they shall be married in the summer."

"What? I never said any such thing," Georgiana stammered, a wave of nausea washing over her. She shook from head to foot, and just when she thought things could not get any worse, the sea of people parted to reveal a very drunk Lord Hugh making his way towards them.

"There she is!" Lord Hugh bellowed, his mark of ale sloshing onto the ice beneath him as he staggered towards them. "The love of my life, Miss Georgiana Darcy!"

Georgiana wanted the ice to open up and swallow her whole. The people around them started gossiping and pointing towards her. Her eyes welled with tears of indignation. "I am no such thing and you know it."

"What's that?" Lord Hugh exaggeratedly put his hand to his ear to hear her better. "Are you saying you are not the love of my life when we are engaged to be married?"

Georgiana hissed, "We are not engaged, Lord Hugh!"

He turned around in a circle, his arms spread wide. "We are to be married in the summer, you know," he called out to the crowd at large.

"You lie!" Georgiana sobbed.

"What?" Lord Hugh spat. "You're jilting me?"

Georgiana then realised the whole thing was staged. Her stomach sank. "How can that be when we were never a couple? Stop lying!"

"How could you?" he bellowed, his face an exaggerated picture of pain. "Why are you ending this, my love? Do not jilt me, Georgiana!" He stretched out his hands towards her.

Georgiana sidestepped behind her cousin.

Richard stepped forward. "That's enough, Lord Hugh. Let's talk about this sensibly."

"Oh, I should have known you would be here," Lord Hugh's words slurred as he turned back around and pointed a wavering finger in Richard's direction. "Has she turned her affections to you now? I wouldn't put it past her." He spat on the ice. "Don't trust her, whatever you do."

Richard strode up to the drunken man and stood almost nose-to-nose with him. "I said that is enough."

Georgiana caught a glimpse then of Richard, the soldier. That was a part of his life she never got to see. She only knew Richard, the gentleman. Now she knew that Richard, the soldier, was just as much a gentleman.

"What do you think you're going to do about it, eh?" Lord Hugh breathed in Richard's face.

Georgiana watched Richard's fists clench and then release. She would not be in the least surprised if Richard was tempted to strike the fellow.

"So confess it. You're in love with her, aren't you?" Lord Hugh pushed on. "You're in love with my fiancée, and she has transferred her affections to you," he bellowed.

"You either stop this foolishness now or I will make known your reputation throughout the country. Is that clear?" Richard growled.

Lord Hugh's eyes opened wide and he laughed. "You seek to sully my reputation?" He pointed past Richard's shoulder directly at Georgiana's face. "It is she who ought to have her reputation sullied for what she's done to me."

"In refusing to marry you, Georgiana has only done what her family would have forced her to do in any case."

Lord Hugh's eyes bulged in their sockets. "You what?" He swallowed and staggered backwards. "Her family would have refused their consent?" he demanded, not quite believing what he was hearing. He snorted.

"That's right." Richard nodded. "Shall we say that we find the idea of your other women and...other children...distasteful."

Lord Hugh stood glowering at Richard, his mouth opening and closing like a fish out of water.

Other children? Georgiana wondered if there was more to the story than Richard had already acquainted her with.

"Damn you, Colonel Fitzwilliam! Who do you think you are?" Lord Hugh grunted. "Do you think you're better than me? Hmm?" He gave Richard's shoulder a shove.

Richard shook his head from side to side sadly. "No, I do not believe myself better than anyone. But I do believe that whomever we decide to marry ought to be able to trust us as much as we would trust them." Richard stepped back to join Georgiana. "Unfortunately, Georgiana knows all about Miss Ainsworth and your son."

Lord Hugh shook with anger and looked as though he was about to explode. He let out a deep roar from somewhere in his stomach and charged at Richard.

Richard, taking hold of Georgiana by the shoulders, merely stepped to the side.

Lord Hugh slipped on the ice, lost his footing, and fell face first down onto the freezing cold surface. The crowd erupted into laughter.

"I think it is time we left," Richard said, taking Georgiana by the arm and leading her towards their carriage.

Georgiana was stunned but admitted more than ever that she was glad to not have thrown away her heart on such a worthless man.

Twenty-Seven

Richard and Georgiana drove home in silence. Georgiana was aware that her cousin kept looking at her. She sensed he was still angry over his exchange with Lord Hugh.

Upon arriving back at Pembroke Square, the pair discovered that Lady Matlock had retired early for the night, leaving them to dine alone.

After changing clothes, Georgiana joined Richard in the dining room. She was still shaken, and Lord Hugh's words reverberated in her mind.

"I'm sorry you had to endure that," Richard finally spoke once the servants had departed.

Georgiana shrugged. "I suppose it was inevitable that some kind of altercation was going to take place." She stirred the soup with her spoon. "I just wish it had not been quite so public. I am certain a good deal of people will think we were engaged."

Richard fell silent, and they ate quietly for some time.

Georgiana put her spoon down when she'd had enough of the soup and viewed her cousin across the table. "I'm just deeply grateful you were there to come to my assistance."

Richard smiled back at her wanly. "And what if I had not been there for you?" Lines appeared around his eyes telling of his deep worry. He cocked his head to the side. "What if I had still been at war and not in England at all? What would have happened then?"

Georgiana swallowed hard. She did not want to even think about what might have happened had Richard not being present this whole time.

"Would you have been coerced into marrying him?"

Georgiana did not have time to reply as Hobbs returned and cleared away the soup bowls. She surveyed the food laid out neatly on the dining table, her appetite waning, and wondered what the future held for her.

"Felicity in marriage is entirely a matter of chance, I have heard it say and personally have observed," Richard's voice was small and weary. "I always dreamt of marrying for love. After all, one is to live with one's spouse until death do us part. However, I am pragmatic. I am the youngest son. I have the small fortune I amassed in the wars with Napoléon, and I know I must marry a woman with money or else condemn myself to a miserly and possibly miserable future."

Georgiana gazed back at him through her eyelashes and her heart went out to him. She wanted to yell, "But I love you and I have a fortune. Won't you think of me?" Instead, she reached out and held his hand across the table.

"I think if there is one thing we have both learnt from our time here in London, it is that we must be sure and know our minds and hearts completely before we consent to marriage." He held her gaze steadily.

She believed she read a deeper meaning within his eyes. "You're quite right."

"I think we both have a lot of thinking to do." Richard pushed his plate away from him. Just like Georgiana, his appetite was gone.

"What do you mean?"

"Whatever decisions we make to secure our future have long-lasting consequences." He gazed into the flame of a candle. "I know I would like to be sure of my heart before I give it away."

"Indeed," she replied, dabbing at the corners of her mouth with a napkin. Georgiana had thought about her future. In recent days, she had spent time pondering where her heart lay. She did not know if she could say she was truly and deeply in love, but, if asked, she could confess that she had a strong and growing affection for the man sitting opposite her. Was it true love? She did not know. The knot in her stomach and the shame that she felt inside told her that she was too young and inexperienced to understand such things. However, when she thought of Richard marrying another woman, she felt as though her heart were being ripped out.

Richard pushed back his chair and rose. "Think I too shall retire for the night."

Before Georgiana could respond, he bowed and took his leave.

Georgiana remained alone in the dining room staring at the empty chair Richard had so recently vacated. She fought against an emotional tide that threatened to force her to run after him. She gripped the arms of the chair. *He is right. I need to think long and hard about my future, just as he does. I need to be certain, beyond a shadow of a doubt, that I do love him.*

Georgiana pushed her own chair back and stood up. She closed her eyes and took a deep breath. *What am I thinking?* she asked herself. *I cannot be sure at all that he returns my affection.*

Again, she felt the crushing sensation of her heart being ripped out. Her eyes stung as she held back the tears. Trying not to run to her room, Georgiana measuredly placed one foot in front of the other and walked calmly upstairs. Once inside her room, with the door closed behind her, she threw herself on the bed, the tide of emotion overcoming her.

Twenty-eight

When Georgiana finally stopped crying, she rose from the bed, washed, and changed into her nightgown. Unfortunately, sleep did not find her that night. Instead, she wrote a lengthy letter to Elizabeth. She described the altercation on the ice, everything that happened before, and her discussion with Richard after.

Georgiana stopped midsentence, the tears threatening to fall again. After composing herself, she touched pen to paper again and scratched her feelings out to her sister-in-law.

My dear Elizabeth, apart from my beloved brother, Richard Fitzwilliam is the most amiable man of my acquaintance. I prefer him above any other man I have ever met. Am I fooling myself again? Am I falling in love with the wrong man?

Richard is everything a man ought to be. He is gallant, respectable, full of wisdom, and undeniably handsome. His steadfast protection of me during my stay here has touched me deeply. He has gone above and beyond what any other cousin would do.

I confess, dear sister-in-law, myself to be smitten. I wish you were here to give me your wisdom.

She ended the missive by sending love to all and signing her name.

She paused and remembered when she danced with Richard here in this house. She was certain then of his regard. The remembrance heated her body and sent that now welcome shock of lightning through her. One thing she understood: when they danced together, he wanted her as deeply as a man can want a woman. She closed her eyes and savoured the sensation firing through her body.

When the light of dawn spread its fingers through the crack in the curtain, Georgiana slipped out of bed, having only slept a little. She crept down the stairs with the intention of placing the letter on the platter to be posted that morning. As she reached the table, she encountered Hobbs.

"I will take the letter for you, Miss Darcy," he smiled kindly at her. "I expect there will be no post for a good few days at least, until a thaw comes."

"Whatever do you mean?" Georgiana frowned.

"It snowed heavily in the night, Miss Darcy." The old man sighed wearily. "I doubt very much even a carriage with sleigh tracks can get through that."

Georgiana darted to the front door and pulled back the curtain that covered one of the full-length windows on either side. She gasped. "That must be at least a foot deep!"

"I believe it is, Miss. Might I suggest you retire to the warmth of your room, and I will have tea and hot water for washing sent up."

Georgiana turned back and smiled at the butler. "Thank you. That would be very nice. It is a little chilly down here."

She scuttled back up the stairs and to her room, where she curled up under a blanket in the armchair before the fireplace and dozed off to sleep. When she woke up, a steaming hot cup of tea was waiting for her.

* * *

Richard barely slept a wink. Each time he closed his eyes, he thought of Georgiana. He tried rationalising his reflections, but each time his heart intervened and told of his ardent love for his young cousin.

Richard had been around long enough to have made a fool of himself in love more than once. He still burned with shame over his infatuation with a married woman. He knew now that it was who she was and what she represented that he loved the most. She was still the most steadfast woman he had ever met. Her unswerving devotion to her husband was admirable.

He then remembered Doña Rocio. The exotic Spanish beauty he rescued from the firing squad knew how to manipulate any man into giving her what she wanted. He would be forever eternally grateful for the fortune she bestowed upon him for saving her life, and he could not blame her for rushing into matrimony with the Andalusian viscount. Rich, beautiful women have to think about their own financial future. If he owned the truth, he was never in love with her to begin with. He was flattered by her attentions and enamoured with her foreign ways and looks.

He rolled over in bed and stared at the ceiling. Within the plasterwork pattern, Georgiana's face stared down at him smiling.

His growing affection for Georgiana was a completely different thing. He had known her from the moment she was born. He remembered her as a sweet, playful child who was painfully shy around strangers. This winter he discovered she had transformed into quite a different creature. She was now an elegant, beautiful, and accomplished young woman. She quite took his breath away.

What Fitzwilliam Darcy would say if he knew Richard was in love with his sister, Richard did not know. Neither did he care. He laughed at himself. Only love produced that devil-may-care attitude that made him want to throw all caution to the wind, dash to her room that minute, and ask her to be his wife.

He rose from the bed, crossed the room, and stared out of the window at the heavily falling snow. He contemplated ringing the bell to forewarn the servants when there was a tap at the door. He opened it to discover Hobbs already knew. He let the chambermaid in to stoke up the fire and returned to staring out of the window.

Come morning, I shall have to know my own mind. Is Georgiana Darcy the woman I wish to spend the rest of my life with? Can I imagine my life without her? How would I feel if she married another?

At the thought, Richard groaned and slumped heavily against the wall. His stomach churned, and he felt sick. It was then he knew his heart and mind were in complete agreement. He loved Georgiana.

Twenty-nine

Christmas Eve

The temperature remained below freezing all that morning. Aunt Henrietta worried that the carollers would not come calling nor would they be able to make it to church for the midnight service. Georgiana hoped the snow would hold off long enough for them to attend.

Soon after breakfast, Richard attempted to catch Georgiana's attention and pull her to the side. "Can we talk?" he asked.

"Of course," Georgiana replied, following him towards the study.

"Georgiana, my dear!" Aunt Henrietta called from the dining room.

"Yes, Aunt?" Georgiana cried back, watching the expression of disappointment on Richard's face.

Aunt Henrietta appeared at the door. "I doubt there will be a single flower to be got in the whole of London today. Would you help me rearrange what we already have in the house?"

Georgiana inclined her head in acquiescence. "Certainly, Aunt. I'll be with you directly."

Satisfied, Aunt Henrietta disappeared back into the dining room. Georgiana looked up into her cousin's face, her heart sunken in disappointment. She relished the chance to spend some time alone with Richard, but now the opportunity was gone. "I'm sorry. Can we talk later?"

He nodded, a sad smile playing on his mouth. "Most certainly. What I have to say to you can wait." He stretched and stifled a yawn. "Besides, I barely slept a wink last night."

"You are not the only one who spent a sleepless night."

Their eyes locked, and in Richard's she saw what she believed were her own sentiments reflected exactly. Hope ignited in her belly.

"I must go to my aunt," she said reluctantly, not moving a muscle.

They remained motionless staring into each other's eyes.

"You best not keep Mama waiting, then."

Georgiana could barely breathe let alone walk away from Richard. Her eyes drifted down to his mouth as she watched it curl up into a happy smile.

Richard closed the gap between them. "Georgiana, I—"

"Georgiana, are you coming?" Aunt Henrietta called.

Unenthusiastically, Georgiana dragged herself away from Richard. "I'm sorry," she whispered as she tripped towards the dining room. "Later, I promise."

As she turned the corner into the dining room, she took one last look at Richard and saw him take a deep breath and sigh.

* * *

Aunt Henrietta kept Georgiana busy for most of the day. A pathway was cleared in the garden down to the great holly bush by the summer pergola. Georgiana put on as many outer layers as possible to make the trek to the end of the garden to cut some holly.

Aunt Henrietta insisted that Georgiana go and cut some sprigs of holly rather than one of the servants. "They would not possibly know what it is we want," she whined. "You and I have both been working on the floral arrangements and decorations all morning. You are the best person to gather the holly for you know precisely what is needed."

Georgiana was tired, and the lack of sleep was catching her up, but she did as her aunt bade. She wondered what Richard was doing as she stepped out of the French doors and crossed the garden, secateurs and trug in one hand and the other desperately clinging on to any bush or tree to prevent her from falling. She suspected that Richard was snuggled up under his thick blankets getting the sleep that she too so desperately needed.

"It's frightfully slippery out here," she called back to her aunt who remained watching from the French doors.

"Then watch your step! What would I say to your brother if you took a fall and broke your ankle?"

Georgiana giggled and waved the secateurs in the air. "Fear not! I am certain he would understand. After all it is in pursuit of the finest holly in the land!"

She could hear her aunt laughing behind her. "I very much doubt that would placate him. Nevertheless, do be careful, my dear."

Once she arrived at the holly bush, Georgiana planted her feet shoulder-width apart for balance and began to search for the best sprigs. In her day, Aunt Henrietta had been a most excellent gardener. She had ensured that both male and female holly bushes had been planted for an abundance of berries. There was plenty for Georgiana to choose from.

Unable to work the secateurs with her mittens on, Georgiana reticently removed them. Unfortunately, this meant that not only were her hands plunged into the freezing air, but they were now open to full attack from the holly itself. She did her best not to get too scratched up, selecting not only sprigs abundant with lush deep green leaves, but some from the other bushes with the brightest and plumpest red berries.

As Georgiana withdrew her hand from the bush, one particularly spiky leaf scratched down the back of her hand. Georgiana winced and clutched it to her. Warm blood trickled down towards her fingers. "Enough is enough," she muttered to herself. "I shall not get lacerated just for a little seasonal foliage for the house."

Georgiana bent down and picked up the trug. As she turned around in her haste to get back to the house, Georgiana lost her footing and slipped on the icy ground. She tumbled backwards, falling awkwardly, and hitting her head on the frozen pathway. She closed her eyes, cringing in pain, and aware that she had let out a high-pitched scream.

The next couple of minutes were a complete blur for Georgiana. Richard's face appeared out of nowhere. Then she had the sensation of being carried. Finally, she was warm and opened her eyes to find she was stretched out upon the settee in the drawing room.

She brushed Aunt Henrietta's hand away from her forehead. "Please don't make such a fuss," Georgiana begged. "I'm not injured, I assure you."

Aunt Henrietta folded her arms across her chest. "I shall be the judge of that, young lady," she stated, pursing her lips. "You took a nasty tumble and hit your head."

Richard, perched on the edge of the settee, added his voice to his mother's. "Mama is right. I saw everything from my bedroom window."

Georgiana looked up at him from her reclining position, and her heart swelled at the thought of him watching her the whole time. "I am quite well." She reached up and touched the back of her head. "Yes, my head hurts, but I do not feel dizzy or nauseated. Other than the cuts to the backs of my hands, I do not believe I have sustained any lasting injury."

Aunt Henrietta huffed. "One can never be sure," she warned, seating herself in the armchair opposite, her face a picture of concern. "Perhaps we ought to send for the doctor. What do you think, Richard?"

Richard sucked the air in through his teeth. "I believe we ought to keep a very close eye on her."

Georgiana made to protest being talked about in the third person, but Richard continued over her.

"I have seen men fall from the roofs of barns and come away unscathed or with little more than a scraped knee."

He turned his attention back to her and she gazed at him lovingly. She liked being under his scrutiny.

"But then again, I've seen men trip over their own feet or fall upstairs and sustain horrendous head injuries."

Georgiana pulled a face at him. "Really!"

Richard snorted. "Honestly, I believe you should rest a little, and I shall keep my eyes firmly fixed on you." He touched the end of her nose.

Georgiana wrinkled said nose and felt the heat rising in her cheeks.

"If you feel the slightest bit dizzy or nauseated, you tell me instantly. Understand?" he said, suddenly serious.

"I understand," she replied, "and I will."

"Or if your vision suddenly gets blurry," Aunt Henrietta added.

Georgiana settled her head into the plump cushion. "I promise, Aunt."

"There is, of course, one positive side to all of this," Richard quipped.

"Oh?" Georgiana asked, her interest piqued.

Richard laughed, his expression one of delight. "Well, as far as I see it, I will now be at the mercy of your every whim."

Georgiana looked deep into his eyes, and she caught the flash of passion that flamed within them. "You mean tea and scones?" she asked innocently, whilst knowing her cheeks burned unashamedly.

Richard coughed and cleared his throat. He twisted his head so that only Georgiana could see his wide-eyed expression. "Of course I meant tea and scones. What else?" He winked, his eyes shone with pure mischief.

Georgiana's stomach somersaulted, and she felt a wave of nausea, but not from her fall, purely out of nerves. *Richard is flirting with me*! she thought, her pulse thudding in her ears. *And in front of his mother!*

"Well, then," Richard slapped his knees, "I'd better ring the bell and fetch madame some tea and scones."

While they waited for refreshments to arrive, Aunt Henrietta watched her niece like a hawk. "Such a pity!" she lamented. "I suppose this means you will not be able to accompany me to church tonight."

Richard spoke for her. "Mama, I believe it is not a good idea for Georgiana to go anywhere this evening. She needs to rest."

“If I have a little nap, I might feel up to it,” Georgiana added feebly.

“Nonsense!” Aunt Henrietta snapped. “I will not have it. Do you remember what I said to you when you went out into the garden?” She did not give Georgiana time to respond. “I said I would not know what to say to your brother if you took a tumble and broke your ankle.” Her voice broke with emotion, and she covered her hand with her mouth. “And now look what has happened.”

Immediately Richard was at her side. He perched on the arm of the armchair and placed his arm about her shoulder. “Mama, do not distress yourself unduly. Thus far, Georgiana is well. She just needs a little rest.”

Georgiana watched on, her eyes now heavy with sleep.

“There is no reason why you should not attend midnight Mass now, is there?”

“No, I suppose not.”

Aunt Henrietta’s reply to Richard was the last thing Georgiana heard before she drifted off to sleep.

Thirty

eorgiana awoke much later, covered in blankets, to a room lit by candles. "How long was I asleep?" she asked.

Richard, who had remained vigilant by her side, smiled warmly at her. "Long enough for your tea to go cold," his smile turned cheeky, "and for me to eat all the scones myself."

Georgiana laughed. "You did no such thing," she said, easing herself up onto her elbow.

"No, I didn't. I saved you one," he replied, pointing to a plate covered with a dome.

"Oh, lovely," Georgiana said, swinging her legs around and sitting up.

Richard passed her the scone and rang the bell again. "Better get you that tea now."

"Where's your mother?" she asked.

Richard picked up the poker and prodded the fire, sending sparks shooting up the chimney. "She's getting ready for the church service."

"Is it that late already?" she gasped, glancing at the clock. Sure enough, it was almost eleven o'clock. "Is she going alone?" Georgiana asked with the scone halfway to her mouth.

"The servants will all be attending."

"Oh." Georgiana hadn't thought about that. At Pemberley, it was usual for the family to travel to the little church by carriage while the servants went on foot.

"She won't be alone, so don't worry." Richard returned to sitting on the end of the settee. "It'll just be you and I this evening."

Alone? The prospect filled Georgiana with both shock and excitement. She sat bolt upright, a thought occurring to her. "I missed dinner."

Richard burst out laughing. "I tell you that you and I will be alone in the house this evening and all you can say is, 'I missed dinner.'"

Georgiana realised what she said and got an attack of the giggles.

"Can I surmise that you are feeling well?" Richard enquired.

Georgiana nodded, composing herself. "Yes, I am." She cocked her head to the side. "But I'm ever so hungry."

That set Richard off again in a fit of laughter that did not stop until Hobbs arrived.

"You rang, sir."

"Yes," Richard replied, forcing his face to straighten. "Miss Darcy has not eaten and would like some dinner."

Hobbs inclined his head. "Of course, sir. We set aside a plate of food. It's keeping warm in the kitchen."

"Very good."

"Can I bring you both anything else?" Hobbs asked. "It's only...we are all heading off to church shortly."

Richard was immediately on his feet. "Right you are. If you would kindly bring Miss Darcy her dinner and us both a fresh pot of tea, that would be wonderful. And," Richard looked around the room, rubbing his hands together, "I think that will be all for tonight. Have a wonderful time."

"Very good, sir. Thank you." Hobbs bowed and turned to leave.

"Oh, and, Hobbs, if I do not see you again tonight, I wish you a very happy Christmas."

Georgiana polished off the last of the scone and watched Hobbs turn back to Richard, a smile brightening up his aged face.

"Why, thank you, sir. And a very happy Christmas to you too."

* * *

As Georgiana sat on the settee, a plate on her lap, Richard watched her eat. That afternoon he had awoken and spied her from his bedroom window. He dressed hurriedly and watched her as she cut holly. He could not keep his eyes off her. He was terrified when she turned back towards the house, slipped on the ice, and tumbled to the ground. His heart was in his mouth as he raced out of his room, down the stairs, and out the back to the garden. He didn't think twice. In an instant, he scooped her up into his arms and, amazed at how little she weighed, he carried her into the drawing room, before placing her gently onto the settee.

His throat was constricted, and he could barely speak. His dear, beloved Georgiana had hit her head, although it soon became apparent that her injuries, if there were any at all, were not grave. She shrugged off all their concerns for her health. Nevertheless, Richard insisted she not accompany his mother to church that evening and rest instead. Despite his honest concern over her safety, Richard had an ulterior motive. He relished the thought of spending an evening entirely alone with Georgiana.

He fought the desire to hold her in his arms and shower her face with kisses. He had not declared himself, and he certainly did not know if she reciprocated his feelings.

She fell asleep, and he watched the rise and fall of her chest as she breathed, not wanting to miss anything in case her breathing faltered and she took a turn for the worse. He struggled against the desire to send for the doctor. He knew better than that. She showed no signs of being seriously injured, and an army doctor had once told him the best remedy for someone who had hit their head was to get plenty of rest.

Now he sat not two feet away from her, watching as she devoured her dinner. "Slow down or you'll give yourself indigestion," he warned.

Georgiana nodded. "I'm so famished."

He reclined and watched her until she was finished; then he put the plate back on the tray. "I'll take this back down to the kitchens, shall I?" he asked.

Georgiana stole a glimpse at the clock on the mantelpiece. "Everyone will have departed by now, won't they?"

"I think I can hear Mama in the hallway now. I'll let her know that you are well. Is there anything else you want from the kitchens?" He gave her a crooked smile. "Any more cakes or scones or the like?"

Georgiana giggled.

"I'll see what I can find." Richard left the drawing room and found his mother, as he suspected, in the hallway. "Mama," he greeted her, kissing her on the cheek.

"Did she eat?" His mother asked, her eyes on the tray in his hands as she tied the bonnet under her chin.

"She did indeed. I believe she is well."

"Thank the Lord!" She raised her eyes heavenward.

"Are you off now?" Richard asked.

"Yes," she replied, placing a hand on his arm. "Will you both be all right here alone?"

"Mama, you will be absent for no more than two hours, I am certain." He kissed her on the cheek again. "Now, go to church. I shall take good care of Georgiana. You can speak with your friends after the service and explain why we had to cancel our little pre-Mass soirée this evening."

Lady Matlock smiled indulgently at her son. "You always think of everything, don't you?"

Richard laughed.

"Well, I shall see you in the morning." She turned towards the door and departed with Hobbs as her escort.

Richard scuttled off down into the kitchens as quickly as he could. He wanted to get back to the woman he loved. He placed the tray down beside the kitchen sink and turned around, surveying the cavernous space, still hot from the activity of cooking dinner. On top of a cabinet on the other side of the room, Richard spied three cake tins. Hastily he crossed the room and open the first one. Inside he found a stash of Cook's famous mince pies. He removed two, replaced the lid, and made his way back upstairs.

He found Georgiana untying her bootlaces. He could have kicked himself. He did not even think that she was wearing boots, and he ought to have removed them for her.

Richard placed the mince pies on the table in front of the settee and was instantly on his knees before her. "Here, let me," he said, taking her boot in one hand and untying the lace with the other.

He slipped off her boot and heard her sharp intake of breath as he placed his warm hands around her ankle. His eyes found hers, and he was not oblivious to her deep breathing, nor with it the rise and fall of her breasts.

Without taking his eyes off hers, he untied and removed the other boot. His heart pounded, and the fire of desire engulfed him. *Now is the time*, he told himself. *Now is the time to tell her how much I love her.* "Georgiana..."

Thirty-One

Georgiana's breath came hard and fast. Richard had removed her boots and was now kneeling before her with his hands on her ankles. Never before had she felt such an intense thrumming of longing throughout her body. She could not have looked away from his warm brown eyes if she tried.

She had glimpsed an instant of the same sensation when they had danced so closely together in that very same room. She felt his arousal then as they moved the bodies against each other, and she suspected from the quickening of his breath now that he felt the same now.

Her heart leapt as he spoke her name. "Georgiana..."

She gasped, sensing what was to come.

"Georgiana," he restarted, "for some time now I have been meaning to speak with you." Richard briefly closed his eyes and she willed him to continue speaking. "I think...I believe...you can be in no doubt of my feelings for you, I believe."

Her stomach lurched, and she wished she hadn't eaten quite so much dinner. "Richard...I..."

"I think you have known it ever since we danced together."

"Yes," she replied, suddenly uncomfortable, agitated, and unable to sit still. She slipped sideways and stood up, rushing behind the settee.

"What is it?" Richard asked, coming to his feet.

"I..." Georgiana could not articulate what she felt. She stared at him, desperately hoping that he could read her mind.

She watched as Richard took a deep breath.

"When I arrived here from the continent, I was taken aback by how much you have grown and matured in the time since we last saw each other. I left a nervous and shy young girl and came back to find a beautiful, accomplished, and confident young woman."

Georgiana clutched her hands to her chest as her heart swelled at his words.

"I have loved every minute spent with you, Georgiana. You have shown me that young ladies in society do not have to be conceited, arrogant, and haughty. You are none of those things." Richard hesitated. "Your concern for my mother's well-being over the running of the household," he outstretched his arm and pointed towards the street, "and last night in the carriage when you spoke about Margaret Ainsworth," he closed his eyes and took a deep, ragged breath. "You touch my heart so deeply."

"I had no idea," Georgiana muttered.

"That's just it, isn't it?" Richard stepped forward. "You didn't do it intentionally. You spoke directly from the bottom of your own kind, compassionate heart. You came up with a solution that will save the family their blushes and allow them to be independent. I am proud of you, Georgiana."

She shuffled her feet nervously on the carpet rug.

"I doubt very much that you are aware of this, but so many women in society would have disregarded Margaret Ainsworth as beneath their contempt. It is quite possible they would have blamed her for being in the predicament she now finds herself in."

"What? That's despicable!" She screwed her face up at the thought.

Richard smiled tenderly. "And that is precisely what I'm saying. Your heart is untouched by coldness and cynicism. You are a wonderful woman, Georgiana Darcy."

All this flattery was almost more than Georgiana could bear. Her face blazed. "Please stop."

Richard took another step around the sofa and towards her, shaking his head. "No. I promise I will never stop telling you how wonderful you are because it is true."

"I only suggested what a decent human being would. What has happened to that young lady is contemptible. Lord Hugh ought to be called to account."

"But he won't be," Richard replied sadly, he held on to the back of the settee.

Georgiana thought of that young girl, now a mother and without a husband, possibly forever. Her eyes stung with tears.

"But now she has a chance of a new life." Richard stepped forward again. "She has reinvented herself as the widow Mrs Murray, and I can assure you that Alex and I will do everything we can in our power to ensure that Mrs Murray does not ever get found out. We will concoct a friendship with the late Mr Murray if needs be."

"Thank you," Georgiana replied, as a tear slipped down her cheek.

"She has a new chance of happiness. Some man may be willing to take on a widow."

Georgiana swallowed hard, unable to speak and knowing he told the truth.

Richard changed the subject. "I cannot tell you how relieved I am that you will not marry that bore of a man."

She sniffed, the tears drying up. "Not half as relieved as I am." She wiped her face with the back of her hand.

Richard reduced the gap between them to only a foot. "Over the last couple of weeks, you have touched my heart so deeply that I am undone."

Finally, Georgiana looked up into his eyes, knowing she would be spellbound by them. "Undone?" she whispered.

"Utterly and completely," he whispered back.

She inhaled judderingly. "I..."

"Yes?" Richard inched forward.

"I don't know what to say."

He reached out and took hold of her hands. Georgiana thought her legs would fail her.

"Then let me say it for you," he said, hugging her hands to his chest. "I love you Georgiana Anne Darcy. I love you with all of my heart."

Georgiana could not believe her ears. She barely heard him above the pounding of her heart. Without her realising it, he eliminated the space between them, pressing his body against hers. She did not flinch, recoil, or step back. She welcomed the feel of his hard, muscular body and returned the pressure in equal measure.

"And if I am not very much mistaken," he muttered, his lips closing in on hers, "you feel the same way about me."

Georgiana's breath caught in her throat as she attempted to reply. "Richard, I..." she breathed.

He smiled and brushed his lips across hers, causing that delicious bolt of lightning to shoot through her body once again. She closed her eyes and gave in to the sensation of his lips teasing hers.

"What were you going to say?" he asked, his hot breath adding to the heat rising within her.

"I love you too," she murmured.

As soon as the words were out, he claimed her mouth with his own. She felt lightheaded, but he surrounded her with his arms and held her tight against him. She slipped her arms around his neck and all the world vanished. The only things that existed for her were Richard, his kisses and touch. She felt the passion and urgency in his kisses rise just as quickly as they did in her.

When he pulled away, she felt the loss of his lips keenly.

"Say it again," he panted, his eyes fixed on her bruised mouth.

"I love you," she replied breathlessly.

Richard laughed, picked her up, and spun her around. "Again," he demanded.

"I love you, Richard Henry Fitzwilliam," she giggled, his felicity contagious.

He set her back on her feet. "I love you too, my dearest, precious Georgiana."

Nothing in the world could have made her happier than she was at that moment, until Richard slipped down onto one knee.

"My darling, Georgiana..."

She gasped and covered her mouth.

"Will you do me the immeasurable honour of consenting to be my wife?"

Now Georgiana knew she had reached the peak of happiness. She nodded with tears streaming down her cheeks. "Yes," she laughed nervously. "Yes, Richard. I will be your wife."

Thirty-two

Christmas Day

Georgiana and Richard spent the next hour cuddled up on the settee, kissing, and whispering about their hopes and dreams for the future. Richard kicked off his shoes and Georgiana covered their laps with the blanket, losing all track of time.

The passion did not wane, and both fought hard to restrain themselves. The temptation was great, but Georgiana delighted in his deep kisses. They were filled with the promise of things to come and a desire she had long hoped for in a husband.

Richard looked up at the clock. "My goodness. Do you realise what time it is?"

"No," Georgiana replied, shifting position and sitting up.

"It's almost two o'clock in the morning."

"We've been talking that long?" Georgiana couldn't believe how quickly the time had passed. She squinted at the clock. Sure enough, it read twelve-fifty.

Richard chuckled, folding up the blanket and pulling Georgiana to her feet. "I don't believe there was much talking going on at all."

She willingly melted into his embrace, savouring the scent of his neck, the taste of his lips still upon hers.

"That means it's Christmas Day," he muttered.

"Yes, it does." She moaned as his mouth found hers, and he kissed her with such devastating passion that her knees buckled.

"Happy Christmas, my darling angel," he breathed, continuing to kiss her so tenderly.

"Happy Christmas, my love," she sighed back.

"Happy Christmas indeed!"

Georgiana and Richard spun around and stood to attention, looking guilty.

"Mother!"

"Aunt Henrietta!" Georgiana took a step backwards.

"So this is what you get up to when I am absent, is it?" Aunt Henrietta stormed towards them and stopped just in front of Richard.

Georgiana feared she would strike him. Instead she leant forward and embraced him.

"I've had my suspicions for days!" she cried out, her face glowing with joy. "I may be old, but I am not out of my wits. There were times I wanted to shake some sense into the pair of you." She glowered teasingly at Georgiana. "So, what does all this kissing mean?"

Georgiana's throat was dry from the shock. She looked to Richard to answer for her.

"Mama, I have asked Georgiana to marry me," he informed her, unable to contain his own delight.

A grin spread across Aunt Henrietta's face. "And what did you reply?" She leant in closer.

"Yes," Georgiana whispered, giggling nervously. "I said yes."

"Huzzah!" Aunt Henrietta cried, pulling Georgiana into a tight hug. "I could not be happier. You are made for each other, but I feared neither of you would think of it, what with the age difference of ten years and all."

"What is that when we are in love, Mama?" Richard asked, picking up Georgiana's hand and kissing the back of it.

"What indeed. It is nothing." She embraced them both at the same time. "Your father, Richard, and your parents, Georgiana, would be so elated at this news. And," she pulled back, her eyes twinkling, "if I remember correctly, there was a difference of eight years between your parents and twelve between dear Thomas and myself."

"I just hope Fitzwilliam will be happy for us and consent," Richard piped in, suddenly filled with nerves.

"Of course he will be," Aunt Henrietta reassured them both and waving away the comment. "How can he not be when he sees how happy you are?"

Georgiana suspected she was right. Her brother was a kind and loving man. He would see in her and Richard the same affection that he enjoyed with Elizabeth.

"Now, if you aren't too excited to sleep, it is time we retired for the night." Aunt Henrietta declared and led the way out of the room.

When they reached Aunt Henrietta's room, Richard asked her, "How long were you standing there watching us, Mama?"

She chuckled as she disappeared into her room. "Long enough, son. Long enough."

Georgiana was reluctant to leave Richard even for one minute, but her door was opposite Aunt Henrietta's, and she knew they could not stay up all night, even if they wished to.

Richard took her in his arms and kissed her deeply. "When the snow is clear enough, we'll travel into Hertfordshire where I will formally ask your brother's permission to marry you."

Georgiana smiled happily, knowing Fitzwilliam would appreciate that. "They will be so happy for us."

Again he kissed her, sending her head into a spin. "Good night," he whispered, his voice throaty.

"Good night," she replied, reluctantly pulling away from him.

She opened the door, slipped inside, then turned and watched Richard walk halfway down the landing and turn back around.

He blew her a kiss. "Georgiana..."

"What is it?"

"Happy Christmas."

Georgiana rested her head against the doorframe, a permanent smile gracing her lips. She could not have imagined, when her aunt invited her to London, that the trip would end in an engagement and her falling deeply in love.

She blew him a kiss back. "Happy Christmas."

THE END

Other Titles

By

Karen Aminadra

PRIDE & PREJUDICE CONTINUES SERIES

Charlotte

Rosings

Wickham

Christmas at Longbourn

Miss Darcy's Christmas

THE EMBERTON BROTHERS SERIES

The Spice Bride

The Suitable Bride

The Searching Bride

THE SOMERFORD SAGA

Gambled on Love

Historical Crime

Relative Deceit: Death in the Family

It's a Man's World: Lettie Jenkins Investigates

Writing as Penny Kane

Polly's Write 'ol Summer

All available now exclusively through Amazon

author.to/karenaminadra

www.karenaminadra.com

Printed in Great Britain
by Amazon

71537375R00187